ISBN 978-1-9990198-0-8 (Paperback Edition)

ISBN 978-1-9990198-1-5 (Electronic Edition)

Some characters and events in this book are fictitious. Any similarity to real persons, living or dead, is coincidental and not intended by the author.

Editing by: Dragonfly Editing

Published by Cauldron Press

info@cauldronpress.online

Visit www.ansage.ca

AETHERBORN

The AetherBorn Saga, Book 1

A. N. SAGE

CAULDRON
PRESS

"Hearts are stronger than swords."
-Wendell Phillips

CHAPTER 1
LITERALLY THE WORST TRAIN RIDE EVER

R uby could feel sweat starting to drip at the base of her back, forming a miniature pool and staining her vintage leather jacket right through her tank. The train had been stuck between stations for twenty minutes and there was no sign that it would start moving any time soon. Ruby was beginning to regret her decision of not snagging the last empty seat when she got on. *This is literally the worst train ride ever,* she grimaced as she rearranged her camera bag. She cast an eye for another people-free pocket on the train without any luck. Looks like it's standing room only for the rest of the ride.

Being just a smidge over five feet tall, Ruby could usually sneak by crowds of people without any issues, and on any other day this claustrophobic train would not affect her at all. Today, however, the weight of two cameras in her bag was starting to take a toll, and she could not wait to get a glimpse of the sun again. Her dark, brown hair was starting to get soaking wet from the heat and she was using the side of her arm to side-swipe it out of her eyes.

I think I live here now. Might as well get comfortable. She shifted her weight from left to right and almost knocked over the young girl next to her with the tripod. She had originally strapped it to her back in hopes of taking up less space, but it had since slid down her back and was now protruding from her waist like the end of a bulky musket. *Twenty-five minutes and counting.*

She lowered her bag to the ground and tried to reach for her camera without causing any harm to anyone in her immediate orbit, but the intention failed immediately. As soon as she bent over, the tripod slid up her back, over her head and made a very direct landing on the lap of the older man sitting across from her.

"I am so sorry!" Ruby perked up and tried to get the three-legged monster off his newspaper, "The stupid thing will not stay put!" Ruby's usually somewhat pale cheeks were flushed with embarrassment. Her only thought now was a quick getaway.

"It's no problem, dear." The man she almost impaled folded his paper and handed her the tripod, "Do you want to take a seat? It might be a while longer, I'm afraid."

Do I ever! She thought; and honestly, if he had asked

her a few minutes later she would have accepted. Luckily for him, she was not yet so tired as to forget her manners entirely.

"Oh, it's ok. I'm sure it will get moving soon. I should probably take advantage of this anyhow." Ruby aimed her lens at the man and took a photo. Her airy giggle made him smile, it's not often a pretty, young girl takes your photo.

Ruby clutched her camera lens and started surveying the train. Her eyes darted through the crowd with sniper-like determination. If she was going to be stuck here, she was definitely going to make the best of it!

So far, Ruby's photography had been, as her professors would call it, an introvert's daydream. She kept to herself when working, and mainly photographed objects that could not talk back. Her most recent series of rotting fruit had even won her a trip to France, which would have been quite exceptional if she had not been expected to spend ten days with a group of strangers. Unlike her parents, Ruby had not inherited the social butterfly gene and had always preferred the company of books, movies, and photos to actual beating hearts. No one was surprised when she was accepted to the photography program at Westerlake University. If there was a career that would allow Ruby to watch life and not actually live it, she'd be all in.

Her first two years at Westerlake were great. Her

professors unintentionally labeled her a "young Man Ray," and she was left to her own devices for the majority of assignments. But this year was different. She had begun to be complacent in her work, and her lack of passion and enthusiasm was starting to get noticed. After their last lecture before Thanksgiving break, her favorite professor asked to meet her in his office.

"Come on in, Ruby." His tone was different than usual. There was no intrigue, no playfulness. Just a straightforward stare and a beckoning to unchartered scolding. His pale blue eyes narrowed, and when he took off his reading glasses, she knew she was in trouble. Professor Tremblay saved that maneuver for his troublemakers.

"How are you, Mr. Tremblay?" She brushed loose pieces of hair out of her eyes. The trouble with having mouse-thin hair was in keeping it from looking like an oil-slick all day. Ruby had gotten used to having bangs in her eyes, but something about this moment seemed serious. She tried to look as carefree as possible, but her nerves were coming through every word, "is everything all right?"

Tremblay was leaning forward on his desk and staring directly at her. Despite being quite small in build, his old age gave him a sense of superiority, which was likely why Ruby valued his opinion of her work above all others. You can't mess up when one of the country's best is teaching you. "Everything is fine, Ruby.

I just wanted to have a quick chat to see what your plans are for your thesis. It seems like it's shaping up to be quite interesting."

"It's going good. I'm still trying to figure out the exact direction I want to take with it..." she lied. She had no direction. She actually hadn't even thought about it yet.

"May I offer some advice?" He crossed his arms and continued rapidly without letting her answer, "It might be time to try something different. You seem fairly comfortable with your subject matter. I understand that it is easy to get sucked into doing what you're good at over and over again. But this is a school. This is your one chance to try everything and see what sticks, without repercussions or consequences."

"Ok..." she had no idea where this was headed.

"I have a little assignment for you for over the holidays. Photograph people. Photograph as many people as you can and forget about the fruit, antiques, and abandoned buildings. Can you do that for me?"

Where was this coming from? Ruby had never photographed people. He knew she wasn't comfortable talking to strangers. Why would he ask this of her?

"You look puzzled."

"I am, Mr. Tremblay. I just..." she chose her next words carefully, "I've never been keen on portraiture, sir."

"I know. That's precisely why I'm asking you to do

this." Tremblay leaned back in his chair, his slightly more relaxed posture made Ruby breathe in deeply and lower her shoulders. *He's just trying to help*, she thought.

"Are you worried my thesis will not be good enough?" Her hazel eyes started to take on a deeper shade as they filled with water. She might not have had any idea of what her thesis was but that did not mean she couldn't get defensive over it.

"Not at all! I'm sure it will be as wonderful as the rest of your work! I just don't want you to graduate without having learned it all. Do you think you can try that?"

How could she not try it? When your favorite professor asks you to do something for your own development, you don't say no. Yet, here she was now, forcing herself to interrupt the train ride of the strangers around her, sweating buckets and regretting agreeing to this little project in the first place.

Just a few shots and you can put your camera away.

She ran her lens across the crowd. Focusing on each passenger's face and trying to figure out why they were there. Where they were going? Were they in a hurry? Were they as uncomfortable as she was?

As she scoped the tin tube, her view landed at the back of the train on two men slightly older than she was. *Are they fighting?* She twisted her lens to sharpen the focus as one of the men leaned in closer to the other. He seemed to be whispering something, something that felt forceful and predatory. His scowling jaw locked tight and his eyes gleamed with pure hatred. He grabbed the man next to him by the shoulders. To anyone else watching it would have looked like a friendly pat on the back but Ruby saw better. She could see the fear in his victim's face. Something was wrong here.

She tried to move closer to the two, but she was trapped in place by the crowd. She put up her lens and zoomed in. The attacker reached into his pocket. *What was he getting?* Ruby couldn't see, there were too many people around. She aimed her camera at his hand as it moved out of his pocket and back towards his train neighbor. Something small. *A ring maybe?* Whatever it was, he quickly buried it in his palm and placed his hand on his neighbor's chest. She could see terror forming on the victim's face. His entire body convulsing with fear.

"Hey!" She screamed as loudly as she could. The entire car now shifted their gaze to the awkward, sweaty girl with the camera. "Stop it!"

She lifted the camera to her face again, what was he doing? Something flashed in the viewfinder. She zoomed in closer. *What is that?* There seemed to be marks on the attacker's arms. Some sort of triangles and lines. Glowing blue like a propane fire. *What the hell is that?*

The train shook a bit as the engines started up again.

Some of the lights that were lighting the advertisements across the top of the car flashed briefly and stopped as the train began moving out of the tunnel. Ruby heard a woman's scream coming from the back of the car. She focused her lens at the crowd standing in a circle. Her gaze shifted down at the train floor. The man she saw being attacked was lying lifeless, face down on the ground. She moved her camera around the train trying to find the attacker. Nothing. *How could he get off the train?* Ruby lowered her camera to her side. She looked at the old man in the seat across from her who seemed more interested in the crossword in front of him.

What just happened here? What did she just see?

The train slowly inched towards a stop at the next station. The doors stood steady for a brief moment then opened to let air into the train. People rushed out, pushing each other aside. The crowd carried Ruby out of the train like a wave of water, a tsunami really. She stood on the platform and watched as two officers made their way into the car, with the doors shutting tight behind them.

"Attention passengers. This platform is currently closed due to an emergency situation. Emergency responders are on their way. We apologize for any inconvenience."

CHAPTER 2
YOU'RE GOING CRAZY, RUBY

What a night. Ruby studied her reflection in the mirror. There was no hiding how tired she felt. Her eyes were red enough to be cast in a vampire film, and the color had completely faded from her skinSpending almost two hours in a hot and crowded subway is not exactly the beauty sleep she was hoping for when she left school today.

With her long, wet hair covering most of her pale face she looked like a hot mess She wiped the fog off the mirror and brushed her hair back. The shower helped. At least physically. Ruby had analyzed what had happened on the train the entire walk home, and she was still confused. The paramedics ruled the death a heart attack but that was all the information she could get. It seemed the cops were only interested in speaking with the people directly next to the victim, but even if they'd wanted to question Ruby... what would she have said? That some guy with glowing marks on his arm killed the man with what looked like a ring? Best case scenario, they would think she was a nutcase and escort her off the platform.

Ruby was starting to think they wouldn't be too far off with that diagnosis. The more she played it through in her head, the more she realized how insane it sounded. There is no way she actually saw what she thought she saw. *People don't glow. End of story.*

Chalking it up to being tired, Ruby slipped into her striped pajamas and headed towards the bedroom. The small, two-bedroom apartment she shared with her friend was dark, and the noise of cars zooming by outside made it seem like a train station more than a home. When Ruby first moved to the city, she thought that living downtown, close to school, would be a dream come true, having been used to silence and farmlands growing up. The bustle of Westerlake was inviting and cozy; something about skyscrapers and condos on every corner made Ruby feel like she had finally made a move just for her. She loved being in the middle of it so much that even the dirty streets she walked each morning were little walks of sunshine. So, when they first saw the tiny space above the shops on Queen street, Ruby wanted to move in immediately. While the place was originally built to house only one person, they managed to turn the dining area into another bedroom with a clever arrangement of bookcases and fabrics. Besides, the draw of the voices of the city lulling them to sleep each night was not something Ruby could let go of. She was slightly regretting choosing those sirens right now.

The twenty feet from the bathroom to her room felt like crossing a dessert. She was exhausted and had to use all of her power to raise her feet for each step. Knocking over a book from her bedside table, Ruby fell into the bed with the speed of a dropping cannon ball. Her eyes shut before she even hit the pillow. Rest had finally found her.

THERE IS WATER EVERYWHERE. *The apartment is full of it. Ruby is sitting up in her twin bed, using it as an ark to save herself from submerging. The tide is rising faster as the clear blue liquid reaches the edge of her bedsheets. She could feel heat pulsating through her toes and fingers. An uncontrollable heat that is spreading through her veins, inching closer to her body. As the water rises, the heat intensifies. It's like a game the two are playing, with Ruby being caught in the middle. She sees a spark in her pajamas. Her body is hot enough to blaze. The spark catches the loose threads on her bottoms and ignites faster than a bale of hay in a lightning storm. Ruby feels the flames move up her legs. She watches as embers fly into*

the rising tides. Her room is water and fire and smoke. There is no getting out.

Ruby opened her eyes and looked around the room. Her gaze moved from the grey curtains, across the photographs on the wall, and slowly landed on her legs. No fire here. She sighed a heavy breath out, feeling a bit silly for getting herself so worked up over a nightmare. Still, something just didn't feel right. The dream was too real, she could still feel heat emanating from her palms. *You're going crazy, Ruby.* She rubbed her eyes and jerked herself upright. *Back to reality, you weirdo. Get some work done.*

Making her way to the small desk next to the window, Ruby grabbed the SD card from her camera and started up her laptop. If she could salvage a few shots from today's ride, she could send them off in the morning and be done with the experiment Tremblay had forced on her. She could not wait to go back to shooting fruit! Fruit did not keep you locked up in a subway stop for hours.

Her old laptop hummed and whirred, and Ruby watched the buffer wheel circle endlessly, hypnotized by its motion. How different life must have been without computers. She had always had a fascination with vintage photography. Picturing the romanticism of spending your days in a darkroom, waiting for images to appear as if by magic. A few years before she started her first semester, Westerlake University tore down the darkrooms in the facility, making it impossible for someone like Ruby to experiment with old processes. As almost a rebellion, she stuck to photographing classic subjects, finding settings in the city that resembled historic sites and recreating oil paintings with her digital camera. It worked great until Tremblay's interference.

Ruby dragged the photos from the train ride to the viewer. *There's got to be something in here that could work!* Her small finger clicked the forward pointer image by image. So far, every photo seemed lifeless and too structured. Even the photo of the old man and his crossword puzzle left something to be desired.

She let out an aggravated sigh and was about to delete the folder when she noticed one of the photographs before the accident. The heart attack victim wasn't alone. She wasn't crazy.

Ruby zoomed in to try and see a face, but the attacker was facing away from her. She hadn't been wrong on the train, the victim was afraid, you could see it all over his face. She clicked to the next image and added sharpness to the photo. She still couldn't see a face, but she could see what the attacker pulled out of his pocket. Not a ring like she thought. It was just a rock. Something almost clear with a brilliant sparkle. Like a diamond, and if it was real, this was the biggest diamond Ruby had ever seen.

As she leaned in closer to her screen, her heartbeat sped up. She was almost shaking. All of the images after the diamond appeared were different. The attacker's arms were covered in what appeared to be glowing blue marks. She zoomed in and out to see if this was perhaps a lens flare, but they were there, clear as day. She grabbed her camera and took a shot of her room. Nothing. No marks on this photo, it wasn't her equipment. How else could she explain this?

She heard keys jingling in the door and turned around to see her roommate's curly head of hair rummaging around in the hallway.

"Fish! You home?" Shaylah yelled from the other end of the apartment. When she'd first met Ruby, she thought her full name made her sound like a celebrity from a vintage mystery film and referred to her as a Big Fish for the first few weeks they spent together. Ruby hated the nickname, but over time it stopped fazing her, it was a little inside joke they shared that made her feel closer to Shaylah.

Ruby waited for her friend to take her sandals off. "Shay, you have to come see this."

CHAPTER 3
OPPOSITES MAKE FOR THE BEST OF FRIENDS

Ruby studied Shaylah's face as she flipped through the images. They had been roommates for years now but she still could not get a good read on her. Shaylah flipped her dark, ringlet-like hair back so she could see the screen better, revealing a small butterfly tattoo at the base of her neck. Sometimes Ruby wondered how she didn't topple over with that beehive of curls on her head. Everything about her was loud, from her bright red lipstick to the multi-colored jumper she was wearing. She was convinced that Shaylah's outspoken personality was why they got along so well; everyone knows that opposites make for the best of friends.

You could hear each click of the mouse as Shaylah skipped from photo to photo. While Ruby was used to being silent, this was an unusually long period for her over-the-top roommate not to speak. When they spilled drinks on each other three years ago at the concert, she took one look at Shaylah and knew without a doubt the girl was destined for film. No surprise when she opted for an acting major. Everyone said it would be a waste of her time, but Ruby knew that if anyone could make it in the industry, it was her best friend. She straightened her back and elbowed Shaylah in the arm.

"Well?"

"I mean, it's totes different from your other work..." Shaylah was half smiling. You could see her searching for words, "why the change?"

"You don't see anything weird here?"

"You mean how close you are to this guy's crossword? Yeah. A little stalker-like, no? So, why people all of a sudden? I thought you hated portraits?"

"Not the photographs, Shaylah. Do you see the weird marks on this guy?" She pointed at the symbols. *How is she not shocked by this?*

Shaylah scrunched her nose and moved in closer to the monitor. She looked back at Ruby then back at the screen. *Finally, she gets it.*

"Dude, what am I looking for here? You have to help me out. Is it like a game? Oh! Like those spot the boat or rabbit in the lines or whatever! Fun!"

Ruby pointed her finger at one of the blue triangles. There was a line running through the top of it that reminded her of an abstract mountain sketch. *Is she nuts? It's right there!*

"Yeah, girl, I don't see it. Maybe it's a photo nerd thing." She giggled, patted her on the back, and started walking towards the kitchen. "You want a cup of tea or something? You look pretty out of it. How was class today?"

Ruby's face turned ghost white. She stared at Shaylah with disbelief. How could she not see the marks? They were right there, shining through the screen. You couldn't miss them. Ruby looked back at the images, maybe if she printed them out it would be clearer.

The marks that were just there a second ago vanished. She clicked through the photos, not one had a trace of markings left. Ruby turned off the viewer, then pulled it up again. No marks. Was she seeing things? Could she really be that tired? "They're gone!" she yelled.

"What?" Shaylah peeked out through the open kitchen door. "Did you say something?"

"I... uh... I'm not sure. I think I saw something that wasn't really there? Maybe I'm more out of it than I thought I was."

"Come in the kitchen! I can barely hear you out there!"

Ruby lazily made her way to her friend, pulling up a bar stool and resting her head between her hands on the counter. She didn't feel tired but how else could she explain what she saw before? The marks were there. She was sure of it. Where did they go? Ruby was starting to feel panicked. Something felt very wrong.

"Shaylah?"

"What's up?" Shaylah flipped her hair again. Her hair flip was almost a tick-like staple. She zeroed in on Ruby and plunked a steaming cup of tea in front of her. "You ok?"

"I'm really not sure anymore." She twisted the string from the tea bag around her finger, "I think I'm seeing things."

"What kind of things?"

"Just weird stuff. Marks on people in photos. I thought I was tired before but now I'm not sure. Do you think..."

"Don't even think about it! You're not like her!"

"What if I am though? Grandma was about my age when she started acting odd. What if it's genetic?"

"It's not genetic. It was a complete fluke. You said so yourself, before."

"I know but this is weird. I could have sworn what I saw was real, but then it was just gone. Normal people don't see things that aren't there."

"Normal people don't stay up until four in the morning working on photos every night. Didn't you just say you've been feeling like you've been getting sick or something? I'm sure you just caught the flu. Plus, you're messing around on the computer all day, so that's probably just a bad combo. If anything, you might need glasses."

"I already have glasses."

"Well, you need to start wearing them, then! Or are you afraid Jake won't like them..." She teased. Shaylah knew how Ruby felt about Jake. They'd been friends since they were kids and she had always had a crush on him.

"Shut up!" She tossed a packet of sweetener at Shaylah. "But yeah, you're probably right. I should wear my glasses."

Shaylah bounced around and grabbed a bottle of rum from the counter. She splashed some in her own teacup, winked at Ruby, and started making her way to the living room. "I'm always right, loser. Why don't we put a movie on and have tea on the couch?" If there's one thing Shaylah knew how to do, it was turn every-thing into a party.

Ruby put down her cup on the coffee table and shifted around the couch to get comfortable. She pulled a blanket over herself, even though it was bikini-hot in the room. Something about it made her feel comforted, and she was always running a few degrees colder than everyone else. "Maybe I should go see Dr. Olivian tomorrow?"

"Your childhood doctor? You're still seeing her?"

"Yeah. I know. It's weird. I'll find someone else, later."

"Hey, remember that med student I went to Sushi with? He probably knows a good doctor! Should I text him and ask?"

Unlike Ruby, who quietly pined for Jake's attention, her best friend took full advantage of the dating pool. There were so many dates that Ruby stopped trying to remember their names. They made a deal that if Shaylah ever went on more than three dates with the same guy she had to write down his full name on a post-it note and leave it on the fridge. So far, there were two post-it notes, and Ruby wasn't holding her breath that med school guy was going to make it up there.

"Sure, why not. Ask him later, I'll just go see Olivian tomorrow for now. I'm sure I'm just tired and stressed."

"You want my tea, instead?"

Ruby looked up at Shaylah holding her cup up towards her. It reeked of rum now. Somehow, she'd managed to sneak more booze into it when Ruby wasn't looking. She gave her friend a chuckle and turned back to the television. She'd get some answers from the doctor tomorrow. Tonight, was Zombie marathon night.

CHAPTER 4
SAVED BY THE SANDWICH

"Miss Black? Are you planning on joining us?" Tremblay's sharp eyes stared at her from behind his laptop. Being backlit by the light of the projection screen made him look ominous and more irritated than he probably was.

"Oh. Sorry. Would you repeat the last sentence? I think I'm just coming down with something." An understatement if there ever was one, Ruby was counting down the minutes until the end of class so she could go see Dr. Olivian. What happened last night with Shaylah was bothering her more than she was letting on. How could it not be? She was seeing things. Things that weren't there.

Lots of kids are tired in school, and none of them are hallucinating. Ruby shifted in her seat, straightened her back, and leaned in to show more interest in the class.

She was already on thin ice with Tremblay and zoning out in his class was definitely not going to earn her any brownie points.

"I promise, I'm back now."

"Welcome back. Now, maybe you can enlighten us with your thoughts on last week's reading material."

Oh yeah, he's pissed. Ruby cleared her throat. This can't be happening, she hadn't even read last week's articles. She was supposed to go over them last night but with everything that happened, it completely slipped her mind. She'd need to improvise. Ruby was usually pretty good at thinking on her feet, her dad called her a natural storyteller a few years ago, and it stuck. Something about watching life through a camera lens all these years gave her a good read on what people wanted to see and hear. Telling a story was just like taking a photo, you just had to play to your audience. She took a breath in and was just about to start spinning a tale when...

"Mr. Tremblay! It's lunch time!" One of the students from the back yelled out. He was already putting his backpack on and getting ready to walk out. "It's been lunch for like ten minutes already.

"Right. Saved by the sandwich, Miss Black. We'll continue this tomorrow. Please come prepared next time."

Professor Tremblay was not one to let go of a bone, and Ruby knew she was in a lot of trouble if she didn't act like top student in tomorrow's class. Right now, however, she had bigger things to worry about. If she was going to make it in time for her appointment with Dr. Olivian she had to make a run for it. It was hard enough getting the rest of the day off from her classes, and she wasn't sure if she'd have another chance this week to skip out of school for an appointment. Not with Tremblay on her case.

Ruby grabbed her unopened notebook, pushed it into her backpack and made a beeline for the door. If she could make the next train, she'd be at Olivian's office just in time.

"Miss Black? Do you have a minute?"

She could hear Tremblay calling out to her as she ran down the auditorium steps towards the emergency exit. *Sorry, professor, this will have to wait until tomorrow.* She pushed the touch-bar, the hallway light flooded the projection screen, and she was on her way.

CHAPTER 5
SOMETHING TO ADD TO THE DIAGNOSIS

The train car was surprisingly empty for this time of day, so Ruby was able to snag a seat by the doors. She was still shaken from her last train ride. Playing with the buckles on her backpack, she set it on the floor under her feet, there was no way she was taking out her camera in a train any time soon.

The medical center where Dr. Olivian's office resided was all the way across town, so there was plenty of time for Ruby to gather her thoughts. She still had no idea what she was going to tell the doctor when she got there. On the phone, she had mentioned that it was an emergency but was seeing imaginary marks really an emergency? Maybe in the grand scheme of things, considering her grandmother's condition, it may have been, but now that she'd had some time to think about it, she felt like she might have over exaggerated about the dire effect of it all.

I'll just go in and ask her to tell me more about the symptoms grandma had at the beginning. Ruby thought, *nothing wrong with being prepared.*

She opened her eyes, worried she might actually fall asleep and miss her stop. As luck would have it, she'd left the articles she'd missed reading for class at home, so she would have to entertain herself with the advertisements in the car. She'd read these a million times over on her commutes to school, but some of them still made her laugh.

Ruby was smiling at one of the slogans for a fast food chain when she felt her palms heating up. They had formed fists without her knowing and were now burning with the heat of a stove top left on a little too long. Ruby unclenched her fingers and looked around the train. She felt eyes on her, like everyone had been watching. Shaking off the feeling, she started to reach for her bag when she noticed a tall man standing two doors away from her.

Is he watching me? Ruby was sure she was just acting crazy again. Why would some random stranger be watching her on a train?

She grabbed her bag and put it on the empty seat next to her and looked up at him. The man looked down quickly and started fumbling with his phone. *This is definitely weird.*

If there was one thing Ruby had learned from her last train ride, it's that the Westerlake subway is full of weirdos. No need to stick around to see if this guy was stalking her, she'd be better off switching cars just to be safe.

"Next stop, Rossington Circle. Rossington Circle is the next stop. Doors will open on your left."

Perfect! Ruby thought.

She grabbed her bag and walked to the last door in the car. The train inched to a stop and she didn't hesitate when the doors opened, running directly into the next car. The doors closed behind her and she looked through the back window towards her previous seat to see if her observer was still there.

He stood in the same spot he had been in before except this time he wasn't looking at his phone. His gaze was on Ruby, and he watched her with the intensity of a lion watching his prey. She turned around and made her way to the back of the car, finding a seat behind a group of kids yelling excitedly about some movie they just saw. They were definitely a good cover from her subway stalker.

Ruby spent the rest of the ride peeking through the group to see if the man was still there. Each time she looked, he was either on his phone or looking around the train. Was she imagining things again? Last night's train ride had left her paranoid and suspicious of everyone around her.

Her stop arrived quickly; time tends to move pretty fast when you're afraid you're being followed. She slid her backpack onto one shoulder and made her way out of the car. One of the band pins she had tacked to her backpack got caught on her jacket and tore a hole in the leather.

Great! Just great. Like being crazy isn't enough. Running up the subway steps Ruby was starting to feel foolish about making such a big deal over all of this. She was obviously just tired, and her mind was playing tricks on her.

If you weren't being such a drama queen maybe you'd be in a better spot at school and your favorite jacket wouldn't be torn.

The leaves had already started to turn and Ruby's sneakers kicked them like a tiny hurricane as she galloped down the street. She looked to see if there were cars coming her way before jaywalking to the center of the road and that's where she saw him again. The man from the train. He was standing at the subway exit, his eyes trained on Ruby.

She picked up her pace and ran across the street. She was starting to get breathless and dizzy. A few more long steps, and she'd be at the center. Jogging faster, she felt like a trapped gazelle running towards water. Her hand reached for the door handle, and she looked back at the subway exit before pulling it open. He was still there. Stoic and calm. Watching her with a fierce intensity.

Ruby ran into the safety of the medical center and made her way to Dr. Olivian's office.

Well, this is something to add to the diagnosis. She thought.

CHAPTER 6
WHAT WOULD YOU SAY YOUR SYMPTOMS ARE?

"How are you, Ruby? You sounded pretty worried on the phone this morning." Dr. Olivian looked up from her notes and studied Ruby's face. There was nothing visibly wrong with Ruby, in fact, she was in the best shape the doctor had seen her in years. Her skin seemed to have gained some color and her eyes had a sharpness to them that the meek girl had not had since she was a child. "What would you say your symptoms are for... what was it you called it? Stress exhaustion?"

When Ruby called this morning, she was still pretty upset over yesterday's events, struggling to find the words to describe what was happening to her, she mentioned having stress exhaustion as it was the first thing that popped into her mind. After all, a university student who suffers from stress related exhaustion did not sound as crazy as telling her doctor that she was seeing people with strange markings on them.

"I don't even know if that's what it is. I actually have been sleeping fine lately. I just..." Ruby looked around the doctor's small office trying to find a book on one of the shelves that could offer some help with finding her words. The office was filled with medical encyclopedias and statues from Olivian's travels, nothing that could help Ruby at the moment. "I'm not feeling myself lately. Not like I'm sick, just different."

"In what sense, Ruby?" She could see the concern on her doctor's face. Her grey eyes widening behind bifocal glasses. Olivian had been her family doctor since she was a child, and Ruby was sure that she would try to help her at all costs. If only she could get her act together and figure out how to explain what had happened.

"Uhm. I think my mind is playing tricks on me. It's like I see things that are so real and right in front of me. Things that I know can't really be there. But something about them just seems more real than anything else."

Olivian picked up her notepad and started jotting down notes. "Did you see something recently?"

"Sort of. Something happened on the subway yesterday. A man died right in front of me. I was photographing people for school and he just died. The strangest part is that I thought I saw someone attack him. Someone that had some really strange marks all over him."

"What type of marks? Were they tattoos perhaps?"

"They didn't look like any tattoos I've ever seen. Something just felt off and then I started having these weird nightmares and I just... Doctor?"

"Yes?" Doctor Olivian stopped writing and locked eyes with Ruby.

"Do you think I'm the same as grandma?" Ruby's shoulders tensed up as she said the words. If Olivian thought she had the same symptoms as her grandmother she would tell her, right? Or would she simply run tests until Ruby lost her marbles and was institutionalized for the rest of her life? No one ever knew what happened to her grandmother. It's as if she was one person one day and then something just switched, her mind gave up on her, somehow. They did their best to care for her, but it was too hard on the rest of the family. It was like she had no connection to reality.

Doctor Olivian got up from her desk and walked to the file cabinets behind Ruby's chair. She unlocked the bottom drawer and pulled out a file. Ruby could see the name 'Black' written in sharpie across the side. Her grandmother's file. The doctor leafed through the pages slowly. The silence and anticipation were gutting Ruby, she wanted answers.

"Ruby, did your parents ever talk to you about your grandmother's condition?"

"Just that she was about my age when she got early onset dementia. That no one could figure out what was wrong or how to help her, so she was placed in a care facility. Dad was very young when she died. He never talked about her, at least not with me. I guess it's too hard, they were very close, I think. Mom said she killed herself in her room right before he and his dad were coming for a visit." Saying the words made Ruby feel so foolish. There was so much about her family history she didn't know. Her parents were never great at talking about their past.

"Well, that is mostly what happened. Back then, dementia was not treated the same way it is now. There weren't as many technological advances to help us treat mental disorders, and because of that, most disorders got clumped together and labelled. Dementia was the first label to tag someone with hallucinations. Especially when the first symptoms present in a patient younger than twenty-five. What happened to your grandmother was tragic, but we are much more equipped to deal with it now."

"But do you think what she had is hereditary? Could I have it now?"

"Ruby, sweetheart. There is nothing that I see in her files that could signify a hereditary issue. In fact, some of the details of her disorder do not even match what we now know of dementia. Unfortunately, there is no way to know exactly what your grandmother's ailment was, based on the notes in her file." Olivian closed the file and leaned on it, "I am sure that you are simply over-working yourself. Have you had any migraines or severe body temperature changes lately?"

"I've had some headaches and I've been dizzy a bit. Also..." Ruby began to tell her about the hot flashes in her palms then stopped, "nothing extreme actually."

Olivian began to say something but was interrupted by a nurse calling out to her.

"I'll be right back, Ruby."

Ruby watched her walk out of the room. *What details didn't match?* She thought. The doctor said that some of the details in her grandmother's file didn't match up to dementia. And why was she asking Ruby about temperature changes? Did her grandmother have similar symptoms?

She looked back at the doctor who was looking at a chart with the nurse outside of the office. Ruby leaned over the desk and opened the file. She started scanning the pages, a difficult task upside down, but she could get the gist of the wording. At least the ones she could understand. There were mentions of hallucinations, her grandmother's doctors also noted she saw people who weren't there. She saw the words 'hands' and 'flame' in the same sentence but could not make out what it said. She turned the page and that's when her eyes landed on two words that made her heart drop. Right there in her grandmother's file the words 'glowing marks' had been underlined with a question mark written next to them. Had her grandmother seen the same marks she saw in her photos? Ruby was about to turn the page when she heard Dr. Olivian's footsteps outside. She quickly closed the file and settled back in her seat.

"Sorry about that. Where were we?" The doctor looked at the file, reached for it and walked to the file cabinet to lock it back up. "Why don't we schedule a couple of tests just to make sure you're fine?"

"Uhm. You know what? You're probably right. I have been doing too much at school. I'm probably just overworked." Ruby grabbed her jacket and bolted out of her seat. "I will definitely keep you posted if anything else happens."

"Why don't we schedule an appointment for next week just to be sure, Ruby?" Dr. Olivian yelled out, but Ruby was already halfway out of the office.

"Sure, sounds good!" She ran out the door, "I'll call you later to set up a time!"

Ruby had no intention of calling back. Olivian was hiding parts of her grandmother's file from her. Why didn't she tell her that her grandmother saw the same marks when Ruby mentioned her own hallucinations? If she was going to get answers, she'd need a second opinion. She'd have to look into getting another doctor tomorrow, but for now, if she didn't get a move on, she'd be late meeting Shaylah after her class.

With the unease of her meeting with her doctor still

fresh in her mind, Ruby almost forgot about her confrontation with the man on the subway. As she walked out of the medical center, her feet stopped abruptly. She was standing in the middle of the street looking straight ahead to the subway entrance. He was still where she'd left him. His jean jacket buttoned up now, hiding the band tee he was sporting underneath. His eyes on her face, watching her without hesitation.

CHAPTER 7
HELLO, MISS BLACK

Ruby turned on her heels and headed back towards the medical center, watching the stranger walk towards her from the corner of her eye. She definitely wasn't imagining this; she was being followed. She walked speedily past the center and looked back as she turned the corner, he was about a block behind her but still on her tail. Her survival instincts started to kick in, she needed to lose this guy and fast.

Her steps sped up as she scanned the next few blocks. The streets were mainly shops and cafes, too open and not crowded enough. Ruby needed something less obvious if her plan was going to work. She saw the streetlight start flashing and ran across the street before traffic started up again. She could see the man wait at the corner; he wasn't as quick to get across. Ruby moved faster now, towards her destination. The wind had picked up since she first left the subway, and she could feel it's razor-sharp slashes on her cheeks. The museum entrance was just on the next block. This was her chance to make a run for it.

A fast glance back and she could see her stalker across the street, moving quickly towards her. Her heart was almost in her throat, and she was terrified, but this was not the time for panic. She needed to stick to her plan.

Holding her backpack in one hand, Ruby ran up the steps to the museum entrance, her student ID already in her hand. She flashed it to the ticket holder who waved her through. The perks of being a student had finally started to pay off. She ran into the museum and stopped behind a load-bearing column in the main exhibit. It offered the perfect coverage for her small body. Pressing her back tightly against the column she looked back to the ticket line. The stalker bought a ticket and was making his way through the crowd.

Ruby ran out from behind the column, making sure he saw her. She'd been to the museum at least a dozen times in the last few weeks for a school project, so she was sure her plan would work. She could feel his presence behind her as she walked through the exhibit. A sharp right turn at the replica of Ghiberti's gates and the room opened up to a labyrinth of statues. It was a long hallway with larger than life-sized Roman sculptures set in an indiscernible pattern. She threw her backpack on to make sure it didn't give her away and crouched behind a bronze chariot sculpture. If she stayed low enough, she could peek just through the chariot wheels and perfectly see the entrance to the labyrinth.

Her breath was uneven, almost choking her with her own fear. She watched as her stalker moved through the statues looking for her. One glance at the door and Ruby could see the museum guard walking away. It was just the two of them now. The stalker inched towards the chariot, he moved slowly but with determination. Ruby watched quietly as his ripped jeans moved past her hiding place. Taking a deep breath in, she pulled a pen from her backpack and ran around the front of the sculpture. Within seconds she had the pen at her stalkers back, praying he would mistake it for a knife.

She pressed the pen deeper into his sweatshirt. He was younger than she thought, only a few years older than she, but definitely much taller. Then again everyone was taller than Ruby. "Looking for me?"

"Hello, Miss Black." He grinned, bright white teeth showing behind a full set of lips.

"How do you know my name, and why are you stalking me?"

"I'm not stalking you, Ruby. I'm trying to help you." He started to turn around. Ruby pressed the pen tighter to make sure he knew she wasn't kidding.

"Help me how? What do you want?"

What had she gotten herself into? Was this about the subway incident? Ruby was panicking now. This stranger knew her name. He knew where to find her. Who knows what else he knew, maybe no one around her was safe. *Shaylah! Damn it!* Ruby forgot about their plan to meet. *Wait 'til she*

hears about this.

"I need your help, Ruby. *We* need your help."

"What? What are you talking about?" Ruby was enraged, she wanted answers. She hadn't felt safe all day and this guy was going to tell her why.

"You saw something on the subway yesterday, didn't you? Something that didn't quite seem real? Well, you're not crazy, if that's what you might be thinking. I can explain everything, but you'll need to stop trying to kill me with that pen." She could see him smile now. He was very much aware of the fact that she was not going to be able to hurt him.

"How do you know I saw something?"

"I know quite a bit, Ruby. It sounds deranged, I know, but I can help you make sense of what's been happening to you. Can I do that?" He turned back to see Ruby nod quietly. She tucked the pen into her backpack and looked up at his green eyes.

"I'm Liam, by the way." He reached his hand out for a handshake. Ruby put her hand in his and gave it a slow shake. "Now, how about I buy you a coffee?"

CHAPTER 8
FIRE GOD FIGHTING FIRES

T his guy is definitely crazy, Ruby thought, as she listened to Liam try to explain to her what she'd been seeing. She studied his face for any sign of irony or laughter as he spoke, but he was as serious as one can get. *He really believed this stuff.*

Having spent the afternoon running away from Liam, she hadn't had a chance to see him clearly. Sitting here now in the lowly lit coffee shop she realized how attractive he was. Not in that pretentious way other boys in her school were. Liam looked powerful and stoic, his olive-skinned face almost sculpted to a fault. The eyes she first noticed in the museum were filled with knowledge, and his messy head of hair accentuated the chiseled jawline that she now watched intently. He was definitely sure of himself; his attitude was of someone who knew better than most, but Ruby wasn't bothered by it. Somehow, she could feel it wasn't undeserved.

Snap out of it, Ruby. You can't be into this freak. She shook her head to launch herself back to reality.

"This all sounds crazy, right?" Liam smiled, as if reading her thoughts.

"I mean, it's not every day that a stranger tells you there is an underground society of, what was it, elemental beings? So yeah, crazy is an understatement."

Is he for real right now? Ruby started to glance around but stopped when their gaze met. He wasn't kidding.

"Look, I know how it sounds. But just try to keep an open mind. I'm sure you're having trouble explaining some of the things that have been happening around you?"

"Well, yeah. But I've been a little stressed with school lately, so..."

"And how would you explain what you saw on the subway? Were those two men stressed with school also?"

"First of all," Ruby straightened her back and lowered her voice, "how did you know I was on the subway? Do we have classes together? I don't remember seeing you around campus before."

"I'm not in school with you, Ruby. That's what I'm trying to explain here. This isn't some class project. I was on that train, too, and I could see that your expression changed when you looked at those two guys. You saw something different about them, Ruby. Don't try to hide it. That's why I had to find out more about you. We rarely know others who are like us unless they make themselves known. I'm just surprised that you're in the dark about this, usually we find out as kids from our parents..."

"Look," Ruby interrupted, "let's just get one thing straight. If this whole thing is real, and I really doubt it is, I am not one of you. My parents are regular people and I am a regular person, not what you're describing here. Whatever I saw... I'm sure there is an explanation."

"Ok. But you don't remember ever having something similar happen before?"

"Obviously, I don't."

"Well, that's odd." Liam scrunched his full lips as if he was trying to solve a complex math problem. "There's got to be a reason why you can see our powers."

That's it, she had to get out of here. She started fumbling with her coffee cup and looking around the room to make sure that there were enough people around to avoid a scene. The place was packed, so this was her chance to get away. "I'm sorry, did you say powers?"

"Yes, powers." He paused. "You probably want to get out of here immediately, right?"

What I want is for him to get out of my head. She thought.

"You understand how you sound, right?" Ruby said

and settled back down. No harm in finishing her coffee, at least. Besides, she couldn't wait to tell Shaylah and Jake about this. Maybe it'll make Jake jealous. Ruby smiled at her own thought, then straightened her face quickly when she saw Liam watching her.

"If it would make more sense, do you want to hear how our kind... sorry, my kind came about? I know I loved hearing this story as a kid, it somehow seemed to make sense. Magic or not. "

"Uhm, ok." Ruby said. Somehow, she knew that even if she said no, he would be telling her anyhow.

"Well, it wasn't always like this. We didn't always hide who we are and our powers. Or at least, that's what we're told now. When I was a kid, I knew I was different. There were things I could do when I got upset or angry that other kids couldn't..."

"Like what?"

"If you stick around long enough, maybe I'll show you." Liam winked and she could feel her cheeks boiling. "I was just, different. My parents never hid who we were. They wanted me to know about my past and why I was the way I was. They used to tell me of a time long before our own. A time when ancient Gods first created the human world. The story goes, that in order for our world to exist, the Gods had to leave earth alone and let its newly made inhabitants live freely. But being the self-loving creatures that they are, they placed a piece of themselves in some of the humans, and with that, the four elemental houses were created. Each of the four houses was gifted with the powers to control and manipulate their respective earthly element: air, fire, water and earth. Unfortunately, they inherited not just the powers of the Gods but also their jealousy and fury, and a war began between the houses that lasted for many years."

"Well, this is realistic..." Ruby huffed, but if she was being honest, it actually sounded like a pretty good story. Liam pretended not to hear her sarcasm and continued.

"Out of fear of being reprimanded by their creators, the four house elders decided to come together and end the war. In order to share their holdings on earth, they forged a sword from the four stones that housed each one of their powers—The Sword of Enuma. For many years, there was peace on the Elemental plane, until one day, the royal son of the house of Air stole the sword in order to gain its power."

Something didn't sound right in this fable. "But why? Wasn't it all working?"

"I guess the need for power always wins out. Anyway, the four house elders found out about his betrayal and decided that sharing power with four very different Elementals would always cause tribulations. After a long deliberation, they came up with a diplomatic plan for peace. Each house was to send forth their strongest warrior to represent them in a battle of strength, wit, and heart. The last two standing houses would unite to carry the burden of the sword's power and have full control of the Elemental plane of existence. When Air and Water won the battle, they locked up the Sword of Enuma and have been ruling over us ever since."

"So, what's the problem, then? I mean, if it's all peaceful, then what happened on the subway?" Ruby didn't believe a word Liam was saying, and she wanted him to know that his facts didn't add up.

"Would you like to live your life under someone else's control? To have no say of what you do, who you can be, who you can love?" His hands formed into fists, and she could see the anger in his eyes. Ruby could swear she could see his eyes darken to a shade of crimson. Her gaze shifted quickly to his hands as he reached across the table and grabbed her arms. "My people will always be powerless against them. We are nothing without the sword."

"Your people?"

"I am a descendant of the house of fire."

"Right... and you're what? Rebelling?"

"Not rebelling, Ruby. We're revolutionizing. We're going to get the sword back and take what is rightfully ours."

Ruby's phone vibrated. She looked down to see Shaylah's picture pop up on the screen. *Crap! I forgot to text her, again!*

She started gathering her things. "Ok. Well, good

luck with that. I hope it all works out. But I really have to run now."

"Please, I know you think I'm nuts, but we could really use your help here."

"What? Me? Why? I don't have these powers or whatever you call them. How can I possibly help you and your, what was it, half-God friends?" She made sure the last part sounded as sarcastic as possible.

"You can see us, Ruby. All of us. I saw how you watched what happened on the subway. You knew those two weren't human, and if you can see them, that means you can maybe see others. If we know who Air and Water are, we can find out where the sword is kept. We can catch them off guard!"

"Listen, honestly, this is really weird. I told you I would hear you out and if I did, you'd leave me alone. Now, I heard your little story and I'm going to get out of here. I expect you not to follow me. We had a deal."

"Will you at least take my card in case you change your mind?"

"Sure. Ok."

Ruby reached across the table and grabbed his business card. *Liam Nar. Westerlake Fire Department.*

"Wait, you work at the Firehouse?" She looked at Liam, startled.

"Yes. Shocked they let crazies on the force?"

"No. Just... fire God fighting fire... It's interesting."

Liam smiled. This girl had a sense of humor after all.

"Oh, and Ruby, be careful please. If I could spot you, that means they could, too."

"So, what if they can?" She had already put on her jacket and was beginning to make her way to the door.

"What happened on the subway wasn't an accident. They know about the resistance, and they will stop at nothing to end it. Even murder. That was one of our main fighters they took down, and it only took seconds to kill him. If you see anything else please promise me, you'll call."

"Fine, I promise!" Ruby yelled out. She put his card in her backpack and disappeared down the street, shaking off an image of his eyes as she ran.

CHAPTER 9
SOMETHING IS WRONG

After her bizarre encounter, Ruby could not wait to get home. She called Shaylah as soon as she left the cafe and made up a story about working on a school project, leaving Liam and his deities out of it. She wouldn't even know how to begin explaining the situation without sounding completely insane.

The narrow street leading to the back entrance of her building was darker than usual, and Ruby had just realized that it was already past six. The sun had started to disappear behind the skyscrapers in the distance. She'd better get a move on getting ready if she had any hope of looking decent for movie night with Jake.

"Hi, Ben!" She waved down the street to the owner of the convenience store on the corner. Ruby had spent many a late night running into his store for refills of chocolate milk and beef jerky. When Ben wasn't yelling at his son on the phone, he could be found outside, chain smoking cheap cigars and complaining about the neighborhood. As it turns out, his family had owned the store for three generations, and ever since the big-box businesses moved in, the neighborhood had gone to pieces. At least, that's what Ben made sure to tell people every chance he got.

"Hey," he grunted under his breath and looked back across the street.

Ruby twisted the door handle and ran up the stairs, starting to take her shoes off before even reaching the main entrance. She couldn't wait to spend some time alone with Jake.

A QUICK HOUR and half later, Jake was sitting on the couch, and she was in the kitchen trying to get tomato paste out of her shirt. The plan to look nice for Jake had been overshadowed by her innate clumsiness, and she managed to drop an entire slice of pizza on the brand-new button-down she'd picked up just for tonight.

"This isn't coming out. I'm just going to change really quick!" she yelled and ran past him to her room. Leggings and a tank top it was.

Jake smiled when she came back to join him on the couch. "Well, that's more a movie outfit anyways." He ran the fingers of both his hands through his full, blond hair to brush it back and looked at Ruby. He liked her best when she wasn't trying so hard, when she was just the girl from down the street whom he had known for most of his life. He reached over to the coffee table and grabbed the remote, "So, what are you in the mood for?"

"Uhm, I don't care. Whatever you want," and she meant it. It didn't matter what Jake picked, she'd be spending the night studying his every move more than watching the movie. "What about that horror movie you were telling me about last time? I forgot the name."

"Oh, yeah! Stairway to Hell! It looks pretty terrible, let's do it!"

The two of them had been watching bad movies together as long as Ruby could remember. Long before Ruby's parents moved her to a different suburb, before the tedious senior year of high school they'd spent apart, and well before Ruby realized that Jake was more than just a friend. Or at least she wanted him to be.

Forty minutes into the film and Ruby was getting agitated. She shifted her weight to lean on Jake's shoulder. "Ugh! This is bad, even for us."

Jake's laugh resonated through the living room. He had the octaves of a performer and ever since he chose to follow in his dad's business, Ruby started to realize how energetic he was. His stage-worthy presence was enough to make everyone notice when the two of them entered a room, so there was no shortage of competition for his attention. His trendy fashion sense and slim but muscular build made him look like he'd just stepped out of a magazine. The bright blue eyes didn't hurt either. A long time ago, Ruby used to be bothered by girls throwing themselves at him when they were out together. Now, she took it as a compliment, whatever girlfriends came and went, they had a bond that was unbreakable.

She had always thought that following his brother's death, Jake would be less outgoing. After all, being the eldest, it was Evan who was supposed to take over the family business. He was perfectly cut out for it, Ruby always thought. Almost an identical replica of their father. His death hit the family hard, but she knew it affected Jake the most. He was supposed to go sailing with Evan that day. If he hadn't stood him up to spend time with Ruby, they would have both drowned. The accident always seemed odd to her. The entire Okenos family had always been excellent sailors, so it was strange to hear that the boat hit a rock and sank with Evan trapped inside. She wanted answers for Jake but knew not to press on. Being an only child, Ruby could never understand the sibling bond they must have had. She was certain of one thing, she would always make sure that Jake knew how important he was to her, even if it was as just a friend.

Kicking off his moccasins, Jake reached for Ruby's

camera on the seat next to him and shoved it in her hands. "Movie selfie time!"

They had been following this foolish little tradition since grade school. Ruby could not remember why it started but she had no complaints. It gave her a chance to not feel like a complete creep when Shaylah asked her about all the photos of Jake on her laptop.

She grabbed the camera and leaned into Jake. She could feel his heartbeat through his shirt. *I'll definitely need to photoshop out my blushing, after,* she thought. Trying to keep the camera steady, Ruby made a funny face and pressed the shutter. She could stay in this moment for the rest of her life.

SITTING in her pajamas on the edge of the sofa, Ruby was watching the light from the cars outside zoom past her apartment windows. Shaylah was taking her sweet time getting home, her date must have gone well tonight. No point waiting up for her.

Jake had left right after the movie ended, and while she had hoped he would stay longer, she was pretty tired from the day and was happy to have a few quiet moments alone before her roommate came barging in excitedly with details from her night. She glanced at the camera on the coffee table and smiled. Making an eager grab for it, Ruby began flipping through the photos from her evening with Jake.

She rolled her eyes at the first few, where her hair was in her face and she was mid talking, quickly pressing delete to remove the evidence. It's funny, but when she met Jake all those years ago, she never would have guessed how handsome he would grow up to be. He sure came a long way from that stout little boy with glasses she used to play ball with. Unlike Ruby, who stayed small and slightly awkward, Jake grew into his glasses and developed into the tall hipster she was now so taken with.

As she studied his face in the photo, she could feel her palms get hotter. Her fingers were clammy and there was a sense of vertigo that began to overcome her thoughts.

Something is wrong, she thought. This was how she felt right before she saw the glowing marks on the subway attacker.

Ruby skipped through the photos trying to find some semblance of marks. There was nothing. As she rolled the wheel to move to the next image, she saw the photo start to move. It was as though the image itself was becoming fluid, and movement began to appear in the background. The wall behind her and Jake was dripping with water, slow drips at first and then pouring on their heads. She could see Jake having trouble breathing, struggling to escape the heavy downpour surrounding him. His body was solid, and she could see in his face that he was trying to move but couldn't. He couldn't escape.

The heat in her hands was so intense that steam started to form on them. The steam covered the camera screen as if a ball of fire had been dropped into the water flowing in the photo. Ruby threw the camera away from her and tried to stand up. She made it about an inch off the couch before the room spun out of control. Falling back down, her eyes heavy, she fell asleep.

CHAPTER 10

I THINK WE NEED TO TALK

"Fish! Fish, you ok?" Ruby woke up to the sound of Shaylah calling her name. There was a look of sincere concern on her face. "I've been yelling your name for, like, five minutes, dude. What happened?"

"Oh. I think I just fell asleep." She lifted herself up to sit and put her hand on her forehead. "Maybe I have a fever or something? I'm not feeling great."

Ruby decided to keep the details of why she passed out to herself, for now. After freaking out about the photos the last time, she couldn't very well tell Shaylah that there was another camera incident. Not without sounding like she needed to be committed.

"Ok... Jake left already?"

Oh my God! Jake! Ruby suddenly remembered what she saw in the photo.

"Uhm. Yeah. He left a while back."

"Is everything ok with you two? You seem weird. Or, like, weirder than usual." Shaylah laughed.

"Yeah, it's fine. He has class early and I was pretty tired, anyways. It's honestly fine."

Because saying fine twice in a sentence makes it believable. Good going, Ruby. She grabbed her camera and pressed the play button.

"Oh, pics! Fun! Let me see!" Shaylah leapt on the couch next to her and reached to see the screen. "These are so cute! I swear, Fish, you guys are going to make such cute babies!"

"Geez, Shay. Creepy much? It's not like that." Ruby rolled her eyes. "We're just friends."

"For now. Hey, where are you going?" She shouted, as Ruby got up and headed to her bedroom. "Don't you want to hear about my date?"

"Uh, sure. Yes, of course. I just have to make a quick phone call first."

She could hear her friend making some sarcastic remark as she walked away but didn't bother to stick around for it. What happened tonight was definitely not fine, no matter how much she tried to pretend it was. Something was very wrong and either she was crazy, or Jake was in danger. If something happened to him and she didn't do everything she could to prevent it, she would never forgive herself. She didn't know how to explain what she saw, why Jake was drowning in the photo, but she knew it had to have meant something. A warning of some sort.

She closed the door behind her and pulled Liam's card out of her backpack.

"Hello?" His deep voice cut through the air. Ruby pressed the phone tighter to her ear, suddenly desperate to see him.

"Liam? It's Ruby."

"Well, hello again. I figured I might hear from you soon."

Ruby pictured what he might look like on the other line. His self-assured grin and those emerald eyes. As much as she didn't want to admit it, he left an effect on her. A memory that clung like a loose dryer sheet. Whether he was telling the truth or not, she wanted to see him again.

"Do you know that bar near my school? The Library? Can you be there tomorrow after lunch? I think we need to talk."

CHAPTER 11
ELEMENTAL GODS IN
WESTERLAKE

Regardless of the name, The Library did not house any reading material for its visitors. It was a dingy, second floor pub that was located just outside of the Westerlake U campus. Those who frequented this place did not come here for the atmosphere. They came because the drinks were cheap, the pub was open pretty much twenty-four-seven, and the day-old fries came with free refills. In a nutshell, it was full of art school students, and Ruby's favorite hangout.

Running up the wooden steps, she was starting to regret her decision to call for this meeting. What was she expecting to happen? The stories Liam had told her at the coffee shop were probably nothing compared to the fantastical details she was sure would come to light today. Though, despite her own feelings, Ruby knew she had to hear him out, for Jake's sake.

She peered through the glass entrance. There were only a few people lingering, so they would have no problem finding a booth to sit in. The pub's decor, if decor was a word to describe it, consisted of four booths, a pool table, and a central bar with ten high-top tables surrounding it. The walls were covered in faux wood grain and had a mishmash of crooked frames all around. No matter the time of day, the lights in The Library were dim and there was always a flickering bulb in the hallway to the bathrooms. Ruby smiled as she peeled open the door, she felt safe here.

Despite being ten minutes early, she could see that Liam was already comfortably situated, in one of the booths, and looking at his phone. She dropped her bag on the table louder than was necessary to startle him to attention.

"Morning!" He looked up at her, beaming.

God, he's cute, Ruby thought, then snapped herself back to the conversation, "It's eleven-thirty."

"I know. I had a late night, so it's technically morning for me."

She slid into the booth and dragged her bag from the table to rest in between them. She needed to keep a level head right now and putting some distance between her and Liam was bound to help.

"So, on the phone you said you figured I'd call, why?"

"Straight to business, I see. You mind if I get a drink first?" he was already sliding out of the booth. "You want anything?"

"Uhm. Just a coffee, I guess," she paused, "and some fries!"

Ruby watched him as he walked towards the bar. If Shaylah was here, she would be all over him. He was exactly the type of guy most girls she knew would be drooling over, and as much as she hated to admit it, Ruby could not look away. Her eyes moved slowly across his broad shoulders and made their way down his back.

Keep it professional! Geez. She told herself and shifted her gaze to a random photo on the wall.

"Here's the coffee, they're bringing the fries out soon. The guy said they're making a fresh batch for you."

"They haven't made a fresh batch here since the nineties," Ruby laughed, "it's sort of an inside joke in this place."

"Oh. Well, that's healthy." Liam sat closer to her this time and was in danger of completely crushing her bag. Getting the hint, she moved it to the other side of the booth seat.

"So?" Her eyes locked on his.

"What? Oh, right! How did I know you'd call?

Honestly, it was just a feeling. I figured you'd come around sooner or later once you'd had more incidents with our world, but there was no way to know when I'd hear from you again. I guess I was *hoping* you'd call, so that worked out well."

"But you understand how everything you've said sounds, right?"

"Of course, Ruby. But once you've had contact with our world it's like the doors just open and it's all around you. We see it all the time with new Elementals, once they get their first power, they're hooked!"

"Elementals?"

"Right, sorry. That's what we're called, I guess. I'm not sure where that came from, but it's been this way since anyone can remember."

"So, these powers, how do you know you have them?"

"It's not really something you have. Usually it starts with a feeling, like you're outside of your own body except in this case you're outside of the world in a way. Different Elementals have different sensations but for the most part it has something to do with the house you belong to. Take my house for example..."

"Fire, right?"

"Yes! Exactly! We're known as controllers of heat and flame, so our feeling usually starts in our hands." Ruby remembered the heat that came off her own palms, could she be like him?

"So, what happens after you get this feeling?"

"It usually starts slow. Most of us get our powers when we're just kids so the first step is learning how to control them. I mean, I couldn't tell you how many things I set on fire when I was a kid!" Liam lowered his voice, suddenly realizing how crazy this would sound to anyone who could overhear. "But you learn to be in charge of that. We have a pretty good support system in place."

"Support system?"

"Basically, our parents are pretty good at being open about who we are so we're not shocked when it happens. Plus, we make sure to stick together as much as we can. We have kind of a central area where we can all get together and learn from each other. The older generation teaches the young ones, so we pass on information that way. It's hard sometimes, we've gotten so used to hiding from regular humans that we're always scared of being found out. And you don't want to trust the wrong house, of course."

"Wait, there are wrong houses and right houses?" Ruby furrowed her brow; this was starting to sound way too complicated.

"Not wrong, just not our side. Remember when I told you about Air and Water? Their control over us?"

"Yes..." she vaguely remembered. In Ruby's defense, she got this information back when she thought he was a nutcase, an opinion that was still lingering in the back of her mind.

"Well, turns out that Fire and Earth Elementals actually make a pretty good team. A few generations ago, our great-grandparents made a pact to regain their freedom and that's how the resistance got started."

"So, it's an actual resistance? I thought you were just being dramatic."

Liam laughed, "It's pretty intense, I know. We do our best to give people the option to not join, but most families opt to help. I started training when I was fourteen, I think."

"Like, physically training?"

"Not only that In order to succeed in this, we need to find the sword, but we also need to infiltrate the Air and Water houses to retrieve it. We're getting pretty close, but since we don't know who the Elementals are, it's difficult to pinpoint a location. Basically, we're looking for a needle in a haystack while blindfolded."

"So, that's where I come in, I guess." Ruby couldn't hide the disappointment on her face. He was only interested in using whatever ability she seemed to have.

"Well, hopefully. If you're willing to help. I get this isn't your problem, but you can't very well go back to the way things were now that you know, can you?"

"I mean, no. I guess not." Going back to the way things were was the last thing on Ruby's mind, all she wanted was to protect Jake from all of this. "So, these powers you were talking about, do any of you see things?"

"What types of things?" He leaned in closer, and Ruby could feel the warmth from his body.

"Like something that might happen... Not literally but just like a bad dream. Except not at night." She had no idea how to describe what she saw and was starting to feel foolish even saying anything. Out of the corner of her eye she saw the sparkle of a ruby stone on his right ring finger. Funny, she didn't take him for the jewelry type.

"Did you see something, Ruby? What happened?"

"Well, it's why I called you here actually. The first time on the subway, I saw some weird marks on one of the guys. Like glowing blue triangles with some weird lines on them. They were all over his arm. And I'm pretty sure I saw him pull out some sort of diamond, but I could be wrong."

"So, he was Air house." Liam whispered under his breath. "And you're not wrong. That was a diamond. Elementals can tap into the powers of their house stones to elevate their powers. That's why the sword makes us so much stronger, it's powered by the stones of the original Elemental elders."

And it explains the ring he's wearing. She thought. *Probably a house stone.*

"Uhm, ok, I guess. Anyways, yesterday I was looking at some photos and had... like a vision or something."

"What exactly was it?"

"It was Jake, he was in some kind of danger. It was as if I was watching him die." She cringed at the thought of remembering the vision again.

"Who's Jake?" Liam quickly asked. Was there a touch of jealousy in his voice?

"He's my best friend since we were kids. I would die if something happened to him."

"So, you're saying you can see what's going to happen?"

"I don't know, Liam. You tell me. You're the expert here." Ruby was getting a little annoyed. She was the one that was supposed to be getting her questions answered and not the other way around.

"Sorry. I know you must be scared right now."

"That doesn't even begin to cover it! I was just minding my own business, trying to stay afloat in school, and all of a sudden there are powers, and marks, and Elementals. Some strange guy shows up out of nowhere and tells me he's part of some secret resistance group that I am now somehow involved in. What's worse is that when I try to get answers, I just get more questions added to the list, and now my best friend's life might be in danger!"

Ruby was shaking, she hadn't even realized how frustrated she had become. Her cheeks flushed red as they often did when she became uncontrollably sad. The idea of something happening to Jake made her want to break out in tears but there was no way she was about to let this guy see her that upset. She looked at Liam but his eyes were open wide and looking elsewhere. She followed his gaze to her coffee cup and saw the liquid swirling in a circle. There was a mini tornado in her cup.

"Have you done that before?" Liam asked.

"No, this is new. Wait, are you saying I did that?" Ruby was terrified. Liam reached over and put his hands on hers. The heat from his palms relaxed her and she started to breathe slower. *How did he do that and why did it feel so good?*

"I think so, I can't do anything to water so that must have been all you. I know this is more to add to the pile, but trust me, I will help you. You're safe with me, I need you to know that. I won't let anything happen to you."

"Because you need me for your little plan, right?" she scoffed.

"No, Ruby. Because you're scared and you don't deserve any of this." He squeezed her palms and smiled, "you said you tried to get answers? Don't tell me you went online for this."

"Obviously not. What would I even search for? Elemental Gods in Westerlake?" Ruby laughed, "I went to see a doctor. I thought I was going crazy. That's where you followed me to yesterday."

"So, what happened?"

"That's the funny part. My grandmother was hospitalized for being unstable so I thought it might be something genetic. I told my doctor that, and she assured me that everything was fine but then I read some of my grandmother's file and there were notes there on similar things happening to her. At first, I thought she was just trying to keep me calm, but now I'm not so sure."

"You think she knows more than she's letting on?"

"I honestly don't know what to believe anymore." Ruby looked down at her phone to check on the time. As much as she wanted to stay with Liam, she wasn't getting the answers she needed from him. Jake was still in danger, and she had no idea what the danger was or how to help. "I have to go. I can't be late to class or I'm in trouble."

She threw her phone in her purse and started to get up.

"Will you promise me you'll call me later?" Liam asked.

"Uhm. I don't know." She didn't want to promise anything, a part of her was still hoping she'd wake up from this nightmare. "Just give me some time, ok? This is a lot."

"Will you at least do me a favor and text me if anything strange happens? Especially if you think you're in danger?"

Ruby didn't know what was worse, having her life upside down or having Liam be worried about her. Was he concerned because she was important to his plans, or did he genuinely care for her? She felt uneasy, like he wasn't telling her everything, but if there was any more, she wasn't sure if she was ready to hear it.

"Sure. I promise." She said loudly, as she squeezed through the door. What she needed right now more than anything was schoolwork and a dose of normality.

CHAPTER 12
EXTRAORDINARY AFTER ALL

Ruby spent the rest of her day feeling sick and disconnected. A part of her wanted to forget everything that happened and dive into her classes with the clearheaded determination she had before. Unfortunately, a much bigger part beckoned her to her new reality. A life where Elemental beings were fighting a war beneath the shadows of normality. She rubbed her palms together. The heat from Liam's hands was still lingering on her fingertips.

"Girl! What happened to you?" Shaylah bounced down the hall towards her. Her violet, ostrich feather blazer swung from side to side. She threw her arm around Ruby and drug her along the row of lockers.

"What do you mean?" Ruby shrugged, pushing the feathers out of her nose with her hand.

"You were supposed to meet me for lunch? Remember? 'Cause you were such a tool before and skipped out on me. I'm starting to think you're trying to get rid of me, here."

"Oh, my God, Shay! I'm so sorry!" She knew Shaylah didn't mean it and was just trying to get attention, but she had ditched her friend twice in a row, now. "Something came up and I totally blanked."

"You mean 'someone'?" Shaylah's face looked sneaky, like she was fishing for information she already had.

"Huh?" There was no point in acting clueless, Shaylah obviously knew something but she needed to know how much dirt she had on her.

"I went looking for you at The Library, figured you might have thought we were meeting there. Like usual."

"Oh."

"So... are you going to fill me in?"

"On..."

"Don't act dumb, girl. Who was that guy? It looked like a pretty intense date. Is he from school? I've never seen him here. And trust me, I'd remember him." Her friend's reaction was exactly what Ruby expected it to be.

"He's just a friend, Shay. Calm down."

"I've never seen this friend before..." she was unrelenting.

"Well, he's a new friend. We're working on a project together. It wasn't a date."

"Looked like a pretty hot project..." Shaylah winked and bellowed one of her dramatic laughs.

Ruby started giggling uncontrollably. Something about Shaylah's laughter was absolutely addictive. "Ok, creep. Why didn't you come say hello when you saw us?"

"Oh, you know. I figured if you're finally getting some, I shouldn't play third wheel."

"Geez, Shay. Again, we're just working together. It's not a big deal." She didn't like lying to her friend, but she couldn't very well tell her the truth, and starting to dissect her feelings for Liam now would not help the situation.

"So, where did you find this hottie anyway? He looks older."

"I met him online in a group." Ruby lied, "he works in the field I'm hoping to photograph. And he's not that much older. I don't think."

"Well, good play. You should bring him around campus more often, might make Jake jealous enough to finally make a move." She pushed Ruby with her elbow and almost knocked her off her feet. Shaylah tended to forget how strong her Amazonian body was.

Damn it! Jake! Ruby steadied herself back on her feet. She had completely forgotten to check in on him. What if something had happened?

"Shoot. I have to go pick up a book from my prof really quick. Wanna hang out tonight? We can do wine and face masks? It's been a while." She felt bad, running off on her friend like that, but she needed to call Jake immediately. When she was sure she was far enough away from Shaylah, she picked up the phone and dialed. There wasn't much of a wait before Jake finally answered.

"Hello?" He sounded flustered, "Rue?"

"Hey! How's it going?" she could feel her cheeks blushing as they often did when they spoke.

"Is everything ok?"

"Yeah, why?"

"You never call me. I thought something happened."

"Oh, no, all good. Just wanted to see how you're doing." He was right, Ruby never called him. She was starting to feel quite foolish now.

Just make sure he's ok and get off the phone, she thought.

"I'm good. Just busy. Dad wants me to start putting in some work at the bank so I can get the hang of the family business. Looks like I'll be taking the reins sooner than I thought. He wants me taking over the district pretty much right after we graduate."

"I thought you weren't sure about going into financing?"

"I mean, I'm not. But I don't think I have a choice. The fam has been working in banks forever."

"Yeah, but doesn't mean you have to."

"I know. It's worth checking out, though."

"Jake Okenos. Financial Overlord of Westerlake."
Ruby teased. Jake was definitely downplaying his family's influence. When he said working in banks, what he
actually meant was controlling all of the finances and
goods coming in and out of Westerlake. When they
were younger, she could never imagine her misbehaved
best friend taking control of his family's business. But
lately, Jake had been groomed into a proper young man
who was beginning to resemble his father more and
more daily.

"Ugh, stop. It's not that bad."

"I'm just kidding. It's actually pretty cool. I'm proud
of you, Jake."

"Well, thank you. But don't be proud just yet. I have
to fly to China next month to shadow dad work his
magic. Not looking forward to it at all."

The idea of Jake leaving so soon made her nervous.
What if what she saw had something to do with this
trip? Was he putting himself at risk by going? She
needed to figure out what her vision meant, fast.

"Don't worry. Once you get there, you'll be fine."
She wasn't sure if she was trying to convince Jake or
herself. "I'm sure it'll be more fun than you think."

"Yeah, I guess." Ruby could hear him smiling on the
other end of the line. "Hey, are you around this weekend? I'm feeling like I should redeem myself for that
terrible movie choice the other night!"

"Sure! Just let me know what day." What better way to keep him safe than to stay close to him?

"Great! Let me check with my dad to see if he has anything planned and I'll text you."

Ruby's head was starting to hurt. She still didn't know what her vision meant and now there was a timeline on figuring it out. She couldn't very well go to China with him or glue herself to his side for the rest of his life. Not that she would mind that very much. She needed more information and there was only one place she could think of that could help figure this out. She needed to get Liam to introduce her to the resistance. He said something about older Elementals, maybe they would know what her vision meant.

She picked up her phone and texted Liam's number. If she was going to help Jake survive whatever imminent danger he was facing, she needed to know everything she could about the Elementals and her own role in it all. For the first time in her life, Ruby felt like she might be extraordinary after all.

CHAPTER 13
BUCKLE UP, SISTER

The sun was just coming up when she met Liam early that morning in front of a pawn shop, just five blocks away from her apartment. When she spoke to him last night, Liam said that if she wanted to learn about his kind, she needed to walk in their shoes. She was going to meet the resistance after all. As frightened as she was, Ruby was excited to find out more about them and meet more Elementals. Despite trying to keep a level head about it, deep inside she knew that Liam was telling her the truth about his kind. Maybe she wasn't as crazy as she originally thought she was.

"I thought we were going to this secret lair of yours, not shopping for used jewelry." Ruby smirked when Liam rounded the corner towards her.

"Ok, first of all, keep your voice down please. The

whole point of a secret meeting area is that it stays secret. Second of all, it's not a lair. Think of this place as..." he searched for the right word to describe what he was about to make her witness to, "a community center."

This should be good, Ruby thought and followed Liam into the shop.

The door hit a bell on the way in and the chime startled Ruby. She jumped from the sound and bumped into Liam's shoulder. His hand reached out to hers as if to reassure her that she was safe and she grabbed hold of him without hesitation.

There was an older man at the counter who watched Ruby warily as they made their way to the back of the shop. Was she the first non-Elemental he'd brought here?

They walked towards a rusty, metal door.She heard a buzzer go off as they approached; it was followed by the click of a lock. Liam twisted the handle and as he opened the door, she could see, over his shoulder, a staircase leading to a lower level. The door slammed heavily behind them leaving them covered in a blanket of darkness.

"Almost there." Liam whispered. He fumbled with his hand on the wall and a brief second later flipped a switch. Ruby's eyes widened as she looked down. The metal stairs were illuminated by the blue light from the overhead bulbs and seemed to be never ending. When they finally reached the floor below, they were met by another metal door at the end of the long hallway in front of them, this one much larger in size.

Liam pulled out a card from his back pocket and slid it into the lock. The vastness of the space on the other side was shocking and Ruby looked around, open-mouthed in disbelief. There were hallways upon hall-ways and the entire sub-basement of this tiny pawn shop went on farther than several city blocks.

"But... how?" Was all she could muster to say.

"Oh, right!" Liam laughed, "I sometimes forget most people don't live like us, so this is probably a shock."

"How big is this place? It looks the size of the museum!"

"Twice as big actually." He smirked. She could tell he was proud of that fact.

"Don't the people upstairs know you're here?"

"We own all the buildings in this area. There are entryways like the one we came through throughout the facility, so we don't attract attention. It's just less obvious that way."

"When you say 'we' you mean...?"

"We share this community with Earth Elementals. It helps to have friends in city planning. They built out this entire place and kept it off city records."

"Wait, what?" Ruby leaned on the yellow railing so as to not fall down, she felt like she just set foot on an alien spacecraft, and to be bombarded with more Elemental secrets right away made her dizzy.

"Well, Elementals choose human careers that are close to their house powers. There are instances of a few going rogue but usually it doesn't happen."

"Human careers?"

"Yeah. What they do when they grow up," He smiled, "it's how we blend in. Fire Elementals like me usually go into training-based careers. Cops, military..."

"Firefighters." Ruby interrupted.

"Exactly! Earth Elementals are more nature and space focused, so they end up in things like farming and hospitals and such. Some go into city planning which is how we ended up with all of this." He waved his arm around like he was presenting a prized bull at a rodeo. "There are quite a few of us who have managed to climb up the ladder, which is great for getting resources and funding the resistance. At least, the ones we've been able to recruit."

Ruby's face scrunched into a worried expression. She didn't realize how much of the city had been absorbed by these demi-Gods. What about other cities? Were there Elementals there, too? Questions were running through her mind non-stop.

"So, why can't you recruit more? Don't you need as many people as you can to get this Sword of Puma back, or whatever?"

"Enuma. The Sword of Enuma. And yes, we do, but we don't know who is an Elemental and who isn't until they make themselves known. You're the only one who can do that without the Sword's help, remember?"

How could she forget? After all, she was convinced this was the only reason Liam was showing her any of this.

"So, do you want the grand tour or what?" He reached his hand out.

"Hell, yes!" Ruby grabbed hold of his hand and followed him down the hallway. The heat she felt before was even stronger this time, making her wonder why she didn't feel it with anyone else in her life. Her mind drifted off, but she quickly refocused her thoughts back to reality. Time to find out exactly what she was dealing with here.

The entire facility was made of metal. The walls were metal sheets, the floors were metal grates and even the few chairs sitting out in the hall looked like they were copper. The blue light illuminating the place was bright enough to see everything clearly, and Ruby took the chance to try and memorize everything she saw. She wished she could take her camera out and take some photos but was pretty sure that was against the rules.

They had since turned a few corners and Ruby was shocked to find they were in a completely different area of the facility. "This is one of the classrooms." Liam pointed for her to look through a window.

"They're so young." She said, eyeing a very normal

classroom setting with about a dozen students all between five and eight years of age.

"These guys are the youngest of all of us. It's rare for Elementals to get any showing of powers so young, but sometimes it happens. They're lucky their parents were already part of the resistance, so it was a pretty smooth transition for them." He knocked on the window and waved. The kids all looked up from their books and smiled at Ruby. A little girl in the back of the class lifted up her bangs and made a face, she reminded Ruby of herself when she was young.

"They look like regular kids..."

"They are regular kids, Ruby. They are just able to do certain things that humans can't. There's nothing wrong with them." He seemed to be upset with her comment and Ruby realized how offensive it must have come across.

"Oh, I didn't mean it like that. I just meant that..."

"I know. It's fine. I forget this isn't something you're used to. Don't worry about it."

He pulled on her hand, and she realized she was still holding onto him. *He must think I'm an idiot,* she thought, but it was too late to let go now.

"What's this place?" She asked, as they walked past a window covered by a large metal sheet.

"That's one of the training areas. There are a few those around. The covered ones are for Fire Elementals. Just to be safe."

"Oh. Right. In case you guys set the place on fire or something?" She laughed.

"Exactly. The entire facility was designed in such a way as to protect everyone here from each other's powers."

"That's why the metal everywhere?"

"Yep. Metal, fireproofing, sound-proofing, and other security measures to keep this place operational. See? This is probably the safest place for you in the city." he smiled.

Too bad she can't move Jake in. She thought.

The tour continued for quite some time. Ruby got to see their medical area, kitchen and lunch space, a few more classrooms and training rooms, and was even shown two empty living quarters. It turns out that a lot of the Elementals, Liam included, preferred to stay as close to the resistance as possible and ended up moving in. The rooms weren't large, but they reminded Ruby of the attic in her parents' home, so she actually found them to be comforting.

The entire resistance was designed like a rabbit burrow. Hallways with rooms on either side of them that opened up to larger, central areas. Followed by more hallways and more rooms. If Ruby had a few more hours in the place, she was sure she could memorize the entire layout by heart.

"Oh, come this way!" Liam shouted, and pulled her

towards a tented space in the middle of the next big open area. "This is my favorite part!"

"What is this place?" Her eyes scanned the room as they entered. It was full of plants and botanicals that climbed the walls. Rows of herbs and vegetables lined the tent and there was an overwhelming scent of tropical florals in the air. "It's amazing!"

"About time you came back!" A voice greeted them from behind. Ruby spun around to see a boy her age with the messiest shag of red hair she'd ever seen. He was wearing an outfit that Ruby could swear was made entirely of hemp and seemed to have not shaved since last Christmas. "I see you brought a friend?"

"Zag! Ruby, this is Zag, our little gardening genius." Liam reached out and patted Zag on the back then pulled him in for a hug, "this is Ruby."

"Oh, right. I've heard a lot about you, milady." Zag flipped his long bead necklace around his back and bowed down with a smirk. As he moved closer to her, a whiff of patchouli hit her nose and she almost sneezed in his face. She blinked a few times to get her eyes to stop watering, but her nose was still itchy from the scent.

"All right, that's enough." Liam shoved his friend out of the way, "it's looking great in here!"

"Yeah, man. I got the kiddies working their powers in here now. Some of them can do stuff I never even dreamed of at their age!"

"Zag created a way to use the Earth House powers

to sustain this place by growing vegetation without seeds or sun or water." Liam explained. When Ruby looked up, she realized that there were no sun lamps or connecting hoses anywhere in the greenhouse, but it was flourishing with plant life. "He and his dad are brilliant with this stuff."

"Comes with the territory I suppose." Zag said and ran his fingers through a leafy bush next to him.

"So, you're an Earth Elemental?" Ruby was finally starting to get the hang of their lineage.

"Yep. He gave you a run-down of the place already?

"He sure did. It's pretty cool down here. Totally unexpected. I mean, it seems like you have a whole other city built for yourselves."

"It's not as great as it might seem, you know." Zag looked around the greenhouse "we've been down here for generations. Looking for clues, training our people, forming alliances. Nothing worked. We're still nowhere closer to being free. Or did Liam leave that part out? The part where we're doing all of this just to be able to live without fear. To have a life where we don't have to look over our shoulder every day. To have choices."

"Zag, leave her alone. She doesn't need to hear all this right now." Liam stepped in front of her as if to shield her from his friend's words.

She was so close to him that she could almost hear every quiet breath forming in his chest. She watched the back of his muscular back rise and fall, mesmerized by the movement. Why could she not stop staring at this guy? She needed to snap out of it, and quickly. "It's fine, Liam. I want to hear more. I want to learn." She said, poking her head out from behind him.

"Well, buckle up, sister! You're about to get a crash course in all things Elemental!"

SHE STARTED to follow Zag out of the greenhouse but looked back to see if Liam was behind them. He was still standing where they left him, with obvious concern on his face. Was he regretting bringing her here? It was his idea to use her to help their resistance, he couldn't very well be worried about her now.

FORGET ABOUT HIM, *Ruby.* She urged herself. *You came here for a reason, so stick to it.*

BUT SHE COULDN'T FORGET about him. Whether she liked it or not, he was the only thing that made her feel safe here, and something made her not want to go anywhere without him. She ran back and grabbed his hand.

"YOU COMING?" she said and dragged him towards Zag.

CHAPTER 14
TOMATOES

R uby could feel her temples pulsate. She'd been underground in the resistance for hours listening to Zag's animated attempt at making Elemental history sound exciting. Aside from the blood-stained war story Liam told her about in The Library, the Elementals tended to stay inconspicuous and away from human eyes. What Ruby started to realize, as she heard more about each house, was that they coveted a very controlled living structure There was no allowance of power use and anyone caught using their powers around humans would be dealt with immediately. Ruby did not need to ask what that meant, judging by Liam's and Zag's somber faces, she knew it could only mean one thing: death.

"So, who does this doling out of punishment, exactly? If no one knows who the other houses are in human form?" she asked, not being able to imagine living in constant fear of being herself.

"Who do you think?" Zag rolled his eyes, "the Air and Water Houses. Having the Sword doesn't just mean they can strengthen their powers, it also means they're able to use it to hone in on Elemental activity in the city."

"But..." she interrupted.

"What? This place?" Zag was answering her question before she even finished, "Totally safe. The walls are a mixture of lead and copper so no one can see what goes on down here. Not even those elite inbreds."

"Zag!" Liam shot him a look of distaste.

"Sorry! They're so pretentious. You'd think they earned their spot in society or something while the rest of us are just the help. It's really annoying and you know it!"

"Well, even still, we need to let Ruby form her own opinions. She *is* a guest here after all."

"Wait," Ruby chimed in, "what do you mean by earn their spot?"

"Girl, keep up." Zag laughed and fist bumped her on the shoulder, "You know how we go into professions based on what our houses are best at controlling on an Elemental level?"

"Yes, I know. Liam told me already. So, how do they have to earn their spot?"

"They don't. That's the point. Conveniently

enough, the two houses that have the Sword and hold all the power are the ones that are also in the most controlling professions in the human world. Between Air's involvement in politics and Water's financial influence they are basically in the top tier of society. Human and Elemental."

"So, you're saying that our politicians can be what? Air Elementals? How far up the chain does this go?"

"Who knows? We have no way of actually knowing who they are. Could be as far as the president."

She was starting to understand their frustration. It's like they were labs rats in a maze and had no means of making any real choices for themselves. Ruby had no idea what she would do if someone else was directing how she should live her life. She'd grown up in such a supportive environment that it was difficult for her to picture herself in their shoes. She was sure of one thing though, she would likely react in a very similar fashion.

"You really think the president could be an Elemental?" she asked.

"Honestly, I have no idea. But having the Sword means they have a much bigger grasp on their powers than we do, so, really there is no end of the road for them. Airs can pretty much cut off all the oxygen from the entire city, so I'm sure no one messed with them back in the day when they started moving in on the political ground."

"So, what can Water do, then?"

"They've got the weather cornered. Basically, if you piss one off, they can drop a hurricane on you in no time."

"Wow." She said, remembering the hurricane she formed in her coffee. It must have been a coincidence, there was no way she could have powers from both Fire and Water, could she?

"Oh, and they can move through space using water. That's pretty cool, too."

"Wait, what? Like teleport?"

"Yeah, kind of. Liam's house can do it, too, with fire, but apparently it hurts like hell, so he doesn't try it."

She looked over at Liam to see if Zag was joking around but he seemed to be treating this like regular, run of the mill information. *Do these guys not realize how insane this sounds? I mean teleportation, hurricanes on demand, full political control? This is nuts.*

"Unreal, right?" Liam said. Once again, he was able to get ahead of her racing thoughts and calm her down. She still needed to figure out how he could do that.

"I mean, it's not normal that's for sure!" The more she heard about their kind, the more intrigued she was about how she fit in here. Why did she have the visions that led her here and why was she the only one who could see the Elementals when even they themselves couldn't.

"So, the Sword, if you get it, will give you more power?"

"Not just more power, girl!" Zag exclaimed, "It would give us control back. We wouldn't live in constant fear of someone power-tripping and wiping us all out. We could practice our abilities and pass on our history to our children without fear of being caught. More importantly, we could use our powers to help. I mean, being human is cool and all, but do you know how much more Liam could do if he could help prevent fires before they start, instead of just hosing them down?"

"But what would happen to Air and Water if you get it?"

"Who cares!" Liam burst in, "Let them try living like this for a change!"

Ruby jumped almost an inch off the chair; she was shocked to see this side of him. A brooding, angry side that she wasn't sure she liked very much. His eyes were shining a bright green, and she could almost see his hatred reflected in them. When she looked down, she noticed a red glow coming from below his collar and the tip of a solid triangle shining through.

"What's the symbol for your house, Liam?" She asked.

"Right side up triangle, shaded in. Why?"

Ruby laughed. "Your colors are showing."

"Wait, you can see it now?" Zag ran around the table towards her, "Check me next! Can you see anything? This is awesome!"

"I don't see anything, Zag," she looked back at Liam

and saw his mark was starting to fade slowly, "it doesn't happen all the time. I don't know why it happened this time, even. I didn't see anything on Liam before."

"Well, what changed?" Liam asked.

"I don't know. One minute it was fine, then you got upset and the air just kind of changed a little, it was like I could feel how angry you were. Then the marks appeared."

"Was it the same thing last time on the subway?"

"Uhm. Yeah, I guess."

"Hmm." They looked over at Zag, who was scratching his head and making the messy layers of hair bounce all around his shoulders. "It seems you're somehow picking up on heightened Elemental emotions. Liam was obviously pissed, and the guy on the subway straight up murdered one of us, so that's bound to get some emotions going. That is very interesting."

Zag started darting from one end of the small room to another, mumbling to himself as he did.

"And he's off." Liam smiled. "He gets like this when he's trying to figure things out. Let's go get some food, this could definitely be a while."

They picked up a couple of sandwiches from the kitchen and as Ruby was about to sit down at a lunch table, she felt Liam nudge her lightly towards the door.

"Let's take these to go. This place is going to get packed soon with all the kids out of class. We can eat in the greenhouse."

They made their way through the hallway leading to the greenhouse and Ruby could hear the excited chatter behind her.

"Told you." Liam smiled and sped up his pace.

The greenhouse was particularly quiet and peaceful with Zag not around. She could see why Liam wanted to come here. It was like something out of a movie, the two of them sitting on the floor with their sandwiches, surrounded by wild greenery.

If this was a date, it would be the most romantic date ever. Ruby thought and immediately felt embarrassed.

"You ok?" She looked up to see Liam staring at her.

"Oh, yeah." Her cheeks were burning hot. "Just thinking."

"About what?"

"Just the Sword. And well. everything. What other powers would you have if you had it? Other than teleporting, which is just totally normal by the way."

"Of course. No big deal, I'm sure." He smiled, and she immediately felt herself relaxing. "Well, like Zag said back there, I could have more control over heat and fire which would be very useful in my career. Right now, I can only do the small stuff, like make flames appear and disappear, but with the Sword I can control as far as the sun itself. Oh, and supposedly Fire Elementals can divinate by using fire, because of their innate ability to read people and situations—but that has never actually been proven."

That could be why he's so good at sensing what I'm thinking. Ruby thought. It was beginning to make a bit more sense now.

"What about Zag?"

"Well, if you ask him, he'll tell you he was dealt the worst deal, but that's not actually true. His house can manipulate plant life and agriculture. Plus, they can move anything the earth touches. Even mountains! I think that's a pretty big deal!"

"So, why doesn't he think so, too?"

"Zag really wants to help more on the military side but he's just not a fighter. I keep telling him we need him here to help us figure out where the Sword is, the guy is an actual genius when it comes to city mapping. He won't listen though, keeps asking me to help train him."

"So, what's wrong with that?"

"It's dangerous, Ruby. When I train, I can't be around other Elementals. I could seriously hurt someone. Without the Sword, our powers are all pretty wonky. One wrong move and I could char my best friend to oblivion."

"So, I guess me watching is out of the question?" She knew what the answer would be but still had to try it.

"Absolutely not happening. The closest you're getting to witnessing Elemental powers is this greenhouse. It's just not safe for you otherwise."

Ruby got up and leaned over one of the rows of plantings. She had to admit, this was a pretty amazing accomplishment underground without any resources. Zag was more powerful than he wanted to admit, it seemed.

She ran her palm through the leaves, they felt lush and she could smell the life in them as she moved across the row. As her fingers traced one of the branches, she could feel her fingers cool down. It felt as though she was holding a bag of ice cubes. She wanted to pull away, but something kept her there. She watched as the stem sprung taller in her hand, growing past her arm and to the height of her shoulders. The leaves turned from a pale green to a deep and luscious jade. From the stems, within seconds formed tiny balls. First green then yellowing until they were a bright red.

Tomatoes! Did I just grow tomatoes! She felt like she was dreaming. Touching the red fruit repeatedly to make sure it was real. It was as real as the sandwich she'd just had for lunch.

"Woah!" Liam yelled, and was at her side instantly. "How did you just do that?"

Her smile was slowly dropping. What was once a feeling of wonderment and excitement had taken a quick turn. All she could feel was fear. She reached for the comfort of Liam's hand.

"I honestly have no idea."

CHAPTER 15
IT'S EXACTLY WHAT I THOUGHT

R uby's night was restless with very little sleep, and when she met Liam in front of the pawn shop in the morning, she could not contain her excitement. After what happened last night in the greenroom, Zag suggested she meet with one of the elders. Anything to help her figure out why she now had Earth powers and what any of it had to do with her visions. It was starting to look like her dream about Jake could have more to do with her than with him, which was a relief. She made a mental note to run it by the elder anyhow.

"Ready for today?" Liam was definitely less excited than she was. She needed him to stop being so worried about her, she wasn't some helpless creature.

"I literally could not sleep last night. I can't wait!"

They made the same journey to the back of the shop

and this time Ruby managed to smile at the shop owner, who looked surprised to see her again. If she was going to make it a habit of coming here, she was going to make some friends.

"Morning! Alice is already in the meeting room. Let's go!" Zag was waiting for them at the bottom of the stairs when they came down. "She's pretty excited to meet you, Ruby!"

"Me, too." She smiled; this was her chance to figure it all out.

Alice was sitting at the same round table they'd gathered around yesterday. She wasn't as old as Ruby had anticipated, and she started to wonder why she was considered to be an elder. Ruby had expected a frail woman with grey hair in a bun and enough wrinkles to battle a Shar Pei. The woman she met was likely in her mid-fifties with almost flawless, olive-toned skin. She was fairly tall and had similar features to Liam, with the same piercing green eyes and sculpted nose.

"This is Alice." Liam said, "She's one of the Fire elders and is, essentially, a walking library of Elemental knowledge."

"And your aunt." Alice elbowed Liam in the ribs and laughed.

So, that's where he got those eyes. Ruby thought.

"It's nice to meet you, Ruby. I've heard quite a lot about you. It seems you had a pretty eventful day yesterday." Her eyes were fixed on Ruby's hands as if to make sure they weren't doing any damage. "Is this the first time something like this happened?"

"Is it the first time I grew tomatoes out of thin air? Yeah, I'd say so." She realized how rude that likely sounded, "Sorry. It's just a lot to get used to still."

"I understand, honey. Don't worry about it. It will take time, but we're here for you."

"It's not the first time." Ruby remembered The Library. "I kind of made a coffee tornado the other day."

"Right, at lunch." Liam added as if just remembering.

"Oh, and sometimes when I get angry, my palms get so hot that I feel like I am actually burning. But that could just be stress. I think."

Alice reached over and placed a palm on Ruby's hand as if to check her temperature. "And when they get hot, do you feel lightheaded?"

"Yes! Exactly! How did you know?"

"Ruby, do you mind helping me test a theory really quick?"

"Uhm, sure." Ruby didn't mind helping but she also wouldn't mind knowing what this theory was. Alice reached into her pocket and pulled out a balled-up piece of paper.

"Here you go," she handed Ruby the piece. "Will you squeeze that really tight and think back to something that makes you upset? Is there anything you can think of like that?"

Was there ever! This entire situation made her angry. Jake was in danger; she was apparently a freak with powers and now on top of it all she was tossed in the middle of some war these people had amongst themselves. Just thinking about it made Ruby furious. She could feel her hand get hot around the paper. The tighter she squeezed, the hotter the paper became. Seconds later smoke emerged from her palm. She kept squeezing and getting angrier with each contraction. It was as if the paper was multiplying her anger. Her palm got hotter and hotter until she could no longer hold on. She flicked her hand and tossed the paper across the table. The ball landed in front of Zag, charred to a crisp with embers trailing away from it.

"Holy crap." Zag's mouth was wide open.

"I did that?" She couldn't believe her eyes. How many strange things had she done so far? What was next?

"It's exactly what I thought," Alice walked over and put her arm around Ruby to calm her down. "We haven't seen something like this in a very long time. Definitely not in the last few generations."

"Something like what, exactly? Will someone please tell me what's going on?" Ruby demanded.

Alice turned sharply to Liam, as if to stop him from speaking. Something was going on here, and she was not getting the full story. Ruby felt deflated. Her hopes of finding out more about her role in their world might prove to be more difficult than she thought. More than that, she felt betrayed by Liam, the one person she counted on to have her back, down here.

Fine! If they want to play games, I can play my own! She decided her best bet was just to go along with their act. She was going to use this facility for everything it had to offer and get the answers she needed without their help.

"We'll need to test a couple of more things out, honey. But right now, it seems that you might have all of the four Elemental powers." Alice's face was stern and while she was speaking, she was still looking directly at Liam. "Why don't we go to one of the training rooms?"

She was afraid, and Ruby could see it. No one knew what powers she might have and if she could control them. She should have been afraid, too, but she was more excited than ever. She was one step closer to finding out what her vision meant. Maybe figuring out these powers would put her on the right track to save Jake. At the least, she could be strong enough to protect him from whatever was coming.

"What do we test next?" she asked.

"Well, we know you can control water, earth, and fire so far. What do you say we go see if you can make one of us stop breathing?" Alice smiled. Ruby knew she was joking, but deep inside she was wondering the same thing herself.

CHAPTER 16
NOT A LOT OF TIME LEFT

As it turned out, Ruby did not have the ability to suck the air out of a room. A huge disappointment, as she would have loved to feel like she could be in control if she was ever face to face with an Air Elemental. After a few hours of trying, she managed to fog up a glass turned over on the table. Alice said that Air's powers were the toughest to control, so it might be some time before Ruby would be able to access them.

The idea of being able to control all the elements was starting to sink in with Ruby. She no longer felt like a weakling bystander. If she was able to control each house, she actually had a part to play in this war. What was worse was that she might actually have to choose a side.

This is definitely not what I signed up for, she thought, and her mind immediately jumped to Jake.

She was no closer to finding out what danger he was in, but at least now she felt a bit more capable of protecting him. Her pace quickened, and she ran to cross the street to a tiny Chinese restaurant near school, where Jake sat in wait of their dinner plans. She'd have to make sure to dig deeper with him, maybe he could help her figure it all out without even knowing it.

"Sorry! I was shooting and totally blanked on the time!" She yelled as she dumped her jacket on the back of the chair in front of him. She was tired of lying to people about the Elementals, it was starting to feel like second nature.

"No worries, I ordered the dumplings already."

Ruby loved the fact that their friendship involved ordering for each other. Something about it felt intimate and familiar. It reminded her of why she valued their relationship so much.

"Good, I'm starving!"

"Long day shooting?"

"Yeah. It's been a hell of a week." She eyed the menu and pretended to pick dinner options, better change the subject fast. "What's been going on with you? Did you decide about the business yet?"

"I gave it some thought. Talked to my dad. I think I'm going to go."

"Oh, yeah?" She was starting to panic, not a lot of time left.

"The way I see it, I should at least check it out. I feel he's really counting on me to step in so..."

"But do you want to step in?"

"I have no clue. But it's not like I have any other big ideas, so maybe this is exactly what I'm supposed to be doing. Wait," he grabbed her hand, "what is this? What happened?"

Ruby looked down at her palms. They were swollen and a few blisters had formed on her fingers. She'd completely forgotten about that piece of paper she set on fire. How was she going to explain this to him?

"Oh. Uhm. I kind of accidentally put my hand on the stove before it cooled down. So stupid, I know." She pulled her hands away and put them on her lap under the table. "It's not a big deal."

"Are you sure? That looks pretty painful." He definitely did not believe her. "And both hands?"

"Oh, you know me, such a klutz. It's really fine. Tell me more about the trip! Are you nervous?"

"Uhm. Ok. But you'd tell me if something was going on, right?" He was not letting this go it seemed.

"Of course. Trust me, everything is great." She lied.

"All right. Just, you've been a little off lately. I haven't seen you that much, Shaylah said you've barely been home and now these weird burn marks? It's a little strange, Rue."

"Well, when you put it that way, of course it is!" She tried to laugh to ease the tension, but the sound got trapped in her throat. "I'm just trying to get as much done during this break as I can. My prof has been on me to try new ways of shooting, so I figured I need to really give it my all. Plus, the more I get done during the break, the less I have to do next semester."

"Ok. Well as long as you're fine."

Their food had just started to arrive, and she was relieved to have the intermission. Jake was just about to bite down on a dumpling when his phone rang.

"Hello?" Ruby tried to hear who was on the other end of the line, but she couldn't make it out. "Yeah, I'm just out for dinner right now. Yes, that's right. Hmm. Right. Yes, I know. I know it's important! Do we have to go through with it? And why can't you do it?"

Jake's smile had dropped, and he had an intense look on his face. She leaned in closer, and he pulled back as if to make sure she was not within earshot. He was hiding something. But why? She was trying to piece together what the conversation might be about, but very little information was coming her way. She could have sworn she heard the name Evan on the other end.

"Fine. I said fine, I'll handle it. Bye." He dropped the phone on the table. "Rue, I am so sorry. My dad needs some help in the office and apparently it can't wait. Are you ok if I leave?"

"Oh. Sure. Is everything ok? I thought I heard something about your brother." She knew how that must have sounded. Jake's brother drowned in a sailing accident four years ago, so why would anyone be bringing him up now?

"Just something with the business. I have to go. I'm sorry!" He got up quickly and rushed to the door. "Let me know what the dinner is, I'll cover it! Sorry again!"

She watched him disappear down the street. Something was definitely odd. She hadn't mentioned Evan in years so as not to upset him, but now that she'd brought up his name it was as if Jake hadn't even noticed. He was hiding something and whatever it was could be the thing that would put him in danger. Ruby knew she needed to find out. She picked up her phone and dialed Shaylah's number. If anyone could help get to the bottom of this, it was her.

CHAPTER 17
HANGING OUT AND GETTING
FACE MASKS

"So, we're doing what? Stalking Jake now?" Shaylah was both intrigued and bothered. This was strange, even for Ruby.

"We're not stalking him. I just want to make sure he's ok. He was acting weird and I'm starting to get worried."

Shaylah laughed. "That's exactly what he said about you."

"Yeah. Thanks for telling him I haven't been home by the way."

"Well, you haven't been. Spending all your time with Mister Hottie from the school project?"

"Geez, Shay. You didn't tell him about Liam, did you?" She was really hoping her friend could at least keep some things to herself.

"Of course not. Although, I probably should have so you two can finally admit that you're hot for each other."

"Ok, well, no one is going to do anything unless we figure out what's going on with Jake." Ruby pulled on her friend's sequined sweater and dragged her down the street.

"So, wait, you sure you heard someone mention Evan?"

"Yeah. Weird, right? I mean, he acted like he didn't even hear me when I asked, but I can swear that's the name they said."

"Why would anyone even bring him up? It was so tragic."

"I don't know. That's why I thought it was weird."

"He said he's going to the office?" Shaylah was trying to figure out what Ruby's plan was. "And we're, what? Following him there?"

"Look, Shay. I get it. I sound like a serial killer, but it didn't sound like a business call. Who makes a business call at night? And I doubt his family would be talking about Evan randomly. Something just felt... off."

"Ok." Shaylah said, she didn't sound like she was on board.

"How about this? We go to his dad's office and if he's not there, then we'll know he lied, and I'll have every reason to worry."

"And if he is there?"

"Then drinks are on me tonight."

"Deal!" Shaylah looped her arm under Ruby's, and they walked down the steps to the subway platform.

BY THE TIME they reached the Okenos offices, it was almost ten. The light from the streetlights was casting shadows on the building walls, and Ruby felt as though they were part of some illegal, drug smuggling operation. The more time they spent lurking in the shadows, the less right the entire thing seemed. Why was she spying on her best friend? This was very much unlike her and she felt like she had betrayed Jake somehow by not believing him. The time she'd spent at the resistance with Liam had put too many paranoid thoughts in her head. Not everything was a conspiracy.

Ruby tightened her leather jacket around her chest to keep the wind out. She was just about to tell Shaylah that they should leave when the doors in the office opened and Jake's father, Cyril, walked out followed by Jake himself. Ruby put her arm in front of Shaylah and pressed her into the shadows of the wall. The last thing she needed was for them to be caught here. They watched quietly as the two got into Cyril's black car and drove off. One of the perks of being part of the Okenos family was never having to take the subway. A fact Ruby always made sure to point out when Jake complained about his life. She wouldn't even know what to do with all the money they had.

"See?" Shaylah smirked, "I told you it was nothing."

She felt dumb now and tried to play with her hair to hide her embarrassment. "Weird, I was honestly sure he wouldn't be here."

"Look, if you want, tomorrow is that presentation at the bank that his dad is putting on with the mayor. I know you're shooting it so you won't have time to hang, but I can go with Jake and see if I can pry some low-key info out of him. It'll probably look less creepy coming from me. No offense, babe, but you're, like, way too intense right now." She was right. Ruby would probably say something she'd regret later if she started poking around for answers.

"That would actually be great, Shay. Thank you!"

"How about we chill out for the night? I feel like you could use a break right now."

Her friend was right; a quiet evening at home was exactly what she needed. She smiled and followed Shaylah back to their apartment. She couldn't wait to have a normal night without paranoia or Elementals. Just two friends hanging out and getting face masks.

CHAPTER 18
SOMEONE KNOWS YOU CAN SEE ELEMENTALS

"Fish! Did you leave the window open?" Shaylah pointed up to their apartment when they reached the back door. The window to Ruby's bedroom was wide open and the fire escape staircase was pulled down.

"I don't think so..." Her thoughts were already jumping to conclusions as she ran up the main stairs.

They huddled together as Ruby slowly and quietly opened their front door. Luckily, she'd left in a hurry this morning and had forgotten to turn off their hallway light, so they could clearly see the entire apartment. Everything seemed to be in place, but they were careful walking in, just in case. Shaylah was switching lights on like a maniac as they made their way through the living room towards their bedrooms. Inching closer, Ruby could already see the mess in her room. She nudged Shaylah towards the small bedroom.

"What the hell!" Shaylah yelled out, no longer trying to be quiet.

"Shhh. What if they're still here?" She was scared. Whatever powers she had been practicing did not set her up for any of this. If there was someone still inside, what was she able to do? Throw some toasty paperwork their way?

"There's no one here, Fish. It was probably some creep looking for cash. Check to see if anything is missing."

Ruby walked around her room. It was hard to tell if anything was actually gone. It seemed as though whoever broke in took everything she owned and tossed it upside down. As though they weren't even looking for anything but wanted to make a huge mess to piss her off. Her laptop was still there but the screen was locked.

Someone tried to crack my password. Why?

She reached into her backpack and pulled out her camera; relieved that it was still there.

"Great idea! Take some pics so we can go to the cops or something. This is honestly so stupid. Does it look like anything is gone? Is your jewelry still here?" Shaylah was in full-blown detective mode now, shifting parts of Ruby's bedroom out of her way with a pen she'd found on the floor.

"What are you doing?"

"Not leaving fingerprints. Obviously. It's like the first thing the cops check for." She rolled her eyes at Ruby and continued her examination.

"We live here, Shay. Our fingerprints are, literally, everywhere."

"Right. Well, you know, better safe than sorry. They'd better get these guys!"

"There's no point, nothing was taken. This is so weird. How come your room doesn't look like this?" Ruby was well beyond worried. Was she a target? And if she was, what were they looking for?

She turned on her camera and started taking photos of the room just in case her sitcom watching friend was right and they decided to report this. She moved through the piles of clothes and papers. Zooming in on her laptop screen and moving around the room like a crime scene investigator. She stepped back to take a wider shot and froze. Fear forced her mouth to widen.

"What is it?" Shaylah asked.

"Oh. Nothing. Just taking it all in I guess." She lied. It wasn't nothing. There were Elemental symbols all over her wall. "I'm going to start tidying up really quickly, ok? This is really freaking me out."

Ruby walked over to the window, closed it and locked the latch. She'd have to look into getting some bars installed tomorrow. She grabbed a random piece of paper from the floor and drew the symbols that she saw in her photo. Some were the triangles she'd seen on the subway, but there were more now. Lines running through geometric patterns and odd shapes all around. She was moving quickly to capture the drawings on her phone, her fingers shaking as she dialed.

"Liam?" her voice was panicked as he picked up. "I Just sent you a photo, can you take a look at it?"

"Sure. Are you all right?"

"Just please look at it. Have you seen anything like this before?"

The line went silent, but she could hear Liam fumbling with his phone in the background. She wished he was here with her now. Something about him put her at ease and she knew that if he were here, she would not be as afraid.

"Ruby, where did you see this?"

"In my room. They're all over the wall. Someone broke in today, but nothing was taken." She took a deep breath in and willed herself to relax. "Liam, I'm getting really scared here. What do they mean?"

"You need to get out of that place immediately." His voice was stern and serious, he was as worried as she was. "They're threats, Ruby. Someone knows you can see Elementals, and they know where you live. Probably, someone from the other houses... and you already saw how far they're willing to go. You can't stay there tonight. It's not safe."

"Liam, I am not going to run away from my own home. Shaylah is here. I'm sure whoever did this will not be coming back when we're both home. You said it your-self, they would be in serious trouble if they used their powers in front of a human."

"They don't have to use powers to hurt you, Ruby. You're not as tough as you seem to think. I'm coming over there!"

"You absolutely are not!" she yelled. "I'm not about to start trying to explain to my roommate why some fire-fighter is coming to hang out with us after our house was ransacked. That is completely out of the question!"

"Well, I can't very well sit back and do nothing while someone is threatening you, can I?"

"You want to help, Liam? Why don't you try to help me figure out why I'm having visions randomly, and why I can control all four house powers. Or why I have them in the first place! Also, maybe instead of trying to rush over here and save me like I'm some wounded baby bird, you could put in the effort to find out what my vision about Jake means, and how we can possibly, oh, I don't know, prevent him from dying?" Ruby's palms were heating up. She had better calm down before she accidentally burned the apartment down.

"Ok. Ok. But promise me you will text me regularly, so I know you're not in trouble. And keep your phone nearby."

"Fine. Whatever." She hung up the phone and had to take a few more deep breaths in order to calm down. She hated the idea that he was treating her like she couldn't take care of herself. Somehow, she'd managed to get through life just fine without his Elemental heroism.

She looked up towards the kitchen where Shaylah was already pouring them two very large glasses of wine.

"You need help in there?" Shaylah yelled out.

"Nah. I think I'll get to this after the event tomorrow. After tonight, I kind of just want to get my mind off everything."

"Already one step ahead of you!" Shaylah was walking towards her with two glasses full to the rim. "Let's go in my room, you can crash there for now."

CHAPTER 19

THE ELEMENTALS ARE HERE

The presentation was held in the lobby of the Westerlake Main Bank. Fifty people were already there when Ruby and Shaylah arrived, with more trickling in by the minute. Ruby went straight for the stage to get the best viewpoint; she would have to spend most of her time photographing the presenters and the crowd. She was still shaken up over last night's break-in, but Jake had gone to a lot of trouble getting her this gig and she couldn't very well back out last minute. Besides which, being out of the apartment was a very big bonus at the moment.

She looked back at Shaylah who was already making a beeline for Jake.

Good! Maybe she'll find out what he was up to with his dad last night!

Once the lobby was full of attendees, Jake's father and Mayor Vanti made their way to the stage. Cyril Okenos was as put together as always. His suit screamed wealth and his white hair was styled in a perfect coif. Ruby could see him shuffling through his papers as he walked over to the microphone. He was the polar opposite to her rock-loving dad, no wonder the two never got along. Ever since they were kids, Ruby and Jake did everything to make their parents as close as they were. From impromptu play dates to forced dinners, nothing did the trick. The two families clashed like water and oil. After a while, they gave up on the idea all together.

The mayor, however, was almost a mix of the two. Not as stoic as Cyril but not quite as peace-loving as Ruby's dad. Ms. Vanti looked much better for her age than anyone Ruby had seen, with legs that started from her neck and worked their way down to her five-inch heels. Her waist-length black hair was perfectly straight, and unlike Cyril, she did not come prepared with a speech. Ruby started photographing the two of them as they made their way through the crowd, they resembled a prom couple about to be crowned king and queen.

Slowly shifting her camera to the attendees so she could capture their awe, watching the two like one watches a celebrity on television. Jake's mom, Rhea, was seated just off the stage and holding onto the Vanti twins for dear life. The two young girls looked like they were about to run off screaming, and Ruby assumed that Rhea had been tasked with babysitting while her husband and the mayor spoke.

She scanned the crowd with her camera, trying to capture as much of the event as possible.

Professor Tremblay would be proud! She thought and continued recording every detail of her surroundings. Making her way to the outside wall, she started circling the large group of attendees. Some were taking notes, some were whispering to one another and a few were looking around much like she was, to see who they could spot in the mass of people.

Cyril had just finished speaking on the economic future of Westerlake and how people could get involved and was handing the mic off to Mayor Vanti for her portion of the presentation.

As she moved towards the front of the stage, Ruby noticed a group huddled near the front door. Something felt off about , so she pointed her lens and zoomed in, focusing her lens with sniper-like precision. The two boys were looking around and scanning the crowd while the girl stood between the two, her face fierce with concentration. She could see her shoulders moving up and down and shifted her camera down to the girl's hands. The girl was not taking notes but rather furiously rubbing the palms of her hands together. Ruby could see smoke begin to form at her fingertips.

Something is wrong. There are Elementals here. She thought. She was about to put her camera down and warn the guards when the glass on her lens shattered. She looked up to see one of the boys looking directly at her, his palms ready for the next attack.

CHAPTER 20
COVERED IN ASHES AND DEBRIS

Ruby's head was spinning, and she was starting to feel nauseous from the vertigo. She managed to duck out of the Elemental's sight line but could now hear a panic start to rise in the crowd. The wall and ceiling behind the stage were crumbling and large cracks started to appear in the tiles. She could see the mayor's bodyguards rush to her side, and she was shooing them off in the direction of her children. Rhea was pulling the girls, who were now crying, away from the stage.

The small curtain lining the podium in front of the mayor sparked and just a few seconds later the entire cabinet was on fire. The screams in the crowd got louder as people began to run towards the exit. The event was a stampede of panic, all rushing towards the same door.

Ruby looked back to the spot where the three

Elementals were, but it was now filled with a wave of people pushing each other out of the way. The Elementals were gone.

"Jake! Shay!" She yelled, trying to spot them in the crowd.

Her eyes darted from side to side. Someone pushed by and shoved her hard enough into the wall behind to leave her back paralyzed for a few seconds from the hit. She steadied herself and pushed her way to the front, through the crowd.

A few feet past the stage she could see Cyril pull someone away and knew it had to be Jake. Shay was nowhere to be found. She grabbed one of the stools next to her and used it as a shield to push through the herd. It was easier to get through once people realized she wasn't trying to take their spot to the exit.

"Jake! Jake!" She yelled at the top of her lungs, but between the screams and blasts of collapsing tile and cement, her voice was muffled. She could see Jake struggling to get back to the stage. Why?

Her eyes moved quickly to scan the area and landed on Shaylah's curly hair at the bottom of the stage. Her friend was trapped under a large piece of marble, struggling to get up.

"Oh, my God! Shaylah!" she ran towards the stage. "We have to get out! This whole place is going to collapse!"

She tried to push the tile off Shaylah, but it was too heavy to lift.

"Hang on, let me find something to help!"

Ruby grabbed the stool she'd used to get here and threw it on the ground, shattering some of the pieces loose. She ran back to her friend and prodded one of the broken legs under the tile and began to kick it in order to raise the piece. She just needed to push it up by a few inches so Shaylah could slide out from under it.

"It's too heavy, Fish." Her friend was pushing back tears of fear and pain. "You need to leave right now!"

"I'm not leaving!" she kept kicking. The tile looked like it was starting to lift. Her next kick sent the stool leg flying across the room. She crouched next to Shaylah and grabbed hold of the rock. "I just need to get it loose so you can squeeze out!"

Her tiny feet slid back across the floor as she pushed. Nothing was working.

Think, Ruby! Concentrate!

She squeezed her hands together and felt energy course through them. Placing her palms below the marble, she closed her eyes and thought of every wrong she'd experienced. Every boy who made her cry, every time someone told her she wasn't good enough. She thought about Liam's need to protect her and how it angered her that she needed his help. She thought about everyone who had been lying to her since she found out about the Elementals. Her doctor, Alice, even Liam.

Ruby let out a scream and the marble tile shattered down the center and fell to pieces on either side of Shaylah. She grabbed her friend by the shoulders to pull her up.

"Ruby, how..." Shaylah's eyes widened with intrigue and then closed abruptly. Her body, as heavy as a corpse, fell to the ground making Ruby tumble with her. Without hesitation, she grabbed Shaylah's arms, dragging her towards the exit. The lobby had been almost completely cleared out now. The stage was alight with fire, and the damage to the wall was spreading fast.

A few blazing seconds later, a security guard was by Ruby's side, helping her get Shaylah out of the building. When they finally reached fresh air, she could see the crowd standing across the street, pale faces full of wonder. Covered in ashes and debris.

CHAPTER 21
OTHER THINGS TO WORRY ABOUT

Shaylah's pale face stared back at her and if Ruby hadn't ridden in the ambulance with her, she would never have recognized the figure in the hospital bed to be her friend. Jake watched her while she sat in silence, holding Shaylah's hand. They'd called Shaylah's parents as soon as they got to the hospital, but they were still a few hours away from the city, and she wasn't going to leave her alone.

Her mind was racing. Why were the Elementals there? Why did they attack? She knew the boys were Earth house and the girl used Fire powers, but she hadn't seen them around the resistance. What made them want to hurt all those people? She tried to divinate the answers from thin air which only made her worry more.

"Ruby?" Liam's voice at the door shook her bones.

She was both angry and relieved. Angry that his people did this to her friend, but relieved that he was there with her. There were questions on the tip of her tongue that only he had answers to, but now was not the time for interrogations.

"How did you find me?"

"I heard what happened on the news." His expression told her there was more to that answer, "I called the bank, and they said there were a few people taken to the hospital. So, when you didn't answer your phone, I came here immediately."

"It's Shay," her voice filled with sadness. "She's been like this since we got her out of the building. They said she broke a few ribs and has internal bleeding. The doctors don't know when she'll come to again."

"Ruby, I'm so sorry." He knelt next to her and put his arm around her shoulder. "I wish I had been there with you when it happened."

What exactly had happened? She wanted to ask when she saw Jake's hand reach between the two of them.

"Hi, and you are?" Jake stood there with his arm extended, ready to throw Liam out of the room.

"Oh. Sorry, man. I'm Liam."

He shook Jake's hand as if agreeing to a duel. Even without her visions, she could sense the tension between them. It didn't help that her body started getting chills and her eyesight seemed to have become slightly blurry.

She wanted to stand up and get in between them but there was little strength left in her legs.

"Sorry, Jake. Liam is a..." she still didn't know the best way to introduce him, "a friend. He's helping me on a project."

"What project exactly?"

"Just for school. It's not important." She nodded at Shaylah, "We have other things to worry about, don't you think?"

Jake shrugged and walked closer to the bed; his gaze trained on Liam. He was studying his every move and gesture. This wasn't just dislike or possessiveness, something else was bothering him. Was he jealous?

"Hey, I know you want to stay longer, but when I asked the front desk where to find you, they kind of hinted at the fact that visiting hours are over." Liam was back on the ground now, shielding her from Jake with his broad shoulders.

"I'm not leaving her here alone." She said, annoyed that he would even imply that she would leave.

"Do you think maybe Jack can stay back for a bit? You've been through a lot today."

"It's Jake." She whispered.

"Oh. Sorry. I'm bad with names." Liam was lying through his teeth. He was great with names and she knew it. In fact, there was very little he was bad with, except reading this situation. His crazy world had put her in danger once again. Her friend was hurt and in order to help her, Ruby had to use her powers. If anyone had seen her, she had bigger problems than getting some rest.

"Rue, it's fine. I'll stay." Jake said, "My dad is still finishing up downstairs with the cops. I'll make sure we stay until her parents get here."

"I don't know. What good is it for me to go home right now?"

"What good is it for you to stay here? I'll text as soon as they get here so you know she is safe. He's right, you need to get some rest."

She didn't want to leave. If she could, she would move into the hospital room, chain herself to the bed, and strike until they let her stay. But they were both right, her staying here was not helping Shaylah. She needed to figure out why the attack happened so she could end her involvement with the Elementals once and for all. It was one thing for her life to be put in danger, but she was not going to put up with her friends being at risk. She knew there was only one person in the room she needed right now to make that happen.

"Walk me home?" Her hand reached for Liam to help her out of the chair. "I could use the fresh air right now."

CHAPTER 22
POWERS IN FRONT OF HUMANS

"So, are you going to tell me what happened today or are we just going to be quiet the whole way?" The hospital was not far from her apartment, but Ruby knew that she wasn't looking for the silent treatment when she asked Liam to walk her home.

"What do you want to know?"

Well this is different, she thought, *he's usually a lot more defensive.*

"How about we start with, oh, I don't know... everything?" Snappy was not her strong suit, but everyone was keeping secrets and she was sick of it. "Why were the Elementals there?"

"The resistance got some information about the mayor orchestrating the attack on the subway. Turns out the house of Air is higher than we thought they were."

"So that was, what? Payback?"

"I don't think it was supposed to be payback. I think they went there to send a message. A 'mess with us and we mess with you' kind of thing."

"So, they were resistance?"

"Yes, since they were kids."

"And you knew about this?"

"No! Of course not!" He was angered by her assumption. "No one knew about this, Ruby! You actually think that after all of these years we would let someone just go rogue and jeopardize the entire mission?"

"You're actually telling me that three Elementals from your resistance somehow destroyed an entire building, almost killed hundreds of people, and you all didn't even know it was coming? That honestly seems pretty far-fetched."

"Why? Do you know what everyone around you is doing?"

"I mean, if they were about to try and kill someone, I think I'd have a pretty good idea."

"I don't think they wanted to kill anyone. They just wanted to level the playing field. Show them that we're not afraid. Look, I don't agree with what they did, and Alice and the elders are already working on moving them out of the resistance, but you need to understand that my people are tired of fighting for their freedom. Some of them are restless and young. Not a good combination."

My people. The words rang through her like razors through cloth. He was never going to trust her. As far as he was concerned, powers or not, she was an outsider. She should be happy, easier to cut their world off if she wasn't a part of it. So why was she so hurt by his words?

"So, what about using powers in front of humans?"

"I don't think that was on their minds at all, to be honest." His eyes met hers and he stopped walking, "Why did you ask that?"

"Uhm. Nothing. It's just, Shaylah almost died. She was going to die if I hadn't helped her. I had to do something, so I..."

"Ruby, what did you do?"

"I might have somehow activated more Earth powers to save her."

"What were you thinking? What if someone saw you?"

"What was I supposed to do? Let her die under a rock! Are you kidding me?" She slapped his arm and he stumbled sideways, shocked at her unexpected strength. "Besides, no one saw me. It was just me and her there when it happened, and she was pretty out of it."

"You're not staying alone tonight."

"Yeah. Ok." She laughed, convinced he was kidding. His eyes did not show a hint of a smile. "Wait, are you serious?"

"Of course, I'm serious. Your apartment was just broken into. You were threatened by someone who knows you can see Elementals, and today you used your powers in public. I am not leaving you alone for even a minute."

She wanted to tell him to go home. To leave her alone. To stop pretending to care for her. Instead, she nodded and checked her pockets for the keys. Whether she liked it or not, she was in the middle of a war. With Shaylah in the hospital, it would be nice not to spend the night in the apartment alone. She reached for the familiarity of his hand and pulled back quickly. Shocked at her own actions.

"Don't worry, I'll sleep on the couch." He said, reading her mind as usual.

CHAPTER 23
I'M READY

Ruby's hand is wrapped tightly around the Sword of Enuma. She can feel the weight of the metal pulling her arm down. The energy pulse through the sword and into her fingertips. She can feel its power trickle up her arm, creeping towards her chest. It is a strange feeling, unlike anything she had ever experienced. It is as if she is wrapped in a shadow, her body weightless and encased in darkness.

She does not know where she is. There is no identifying feature in the room to give her an idea of her location. The walls are dripping wet, and the ground is raw dirt beneath her bare feet. She is breathing in slow motion, and each breath out sends fog from her mouth. She feels like a dragon waking up from deep sleep, learning to breathe fire.

There are no exits here. Just wetness, and each of the

four walls encasing her has symbols. Elemental houses glow all around her. She pulls the sword up to her chest, watching the gemstones twinkle in the dim light.

As she points the tip of the sword in the direction of the wall in front of her, the sapphire on the handle shines brighter.

Water House, she thinks and pulls the sword toward the wall on the left of her.

Earth House, she whispers as the emerald begins to light.

She does the same for the other two walls, each illuminating a different stone on the sword. Finishing the rotation, she lifts the sword as high as her thin arm allows and cries out from the heaviness of its weight. She can see all four gemstones gleam in unison. Her body is trembling. This is new power. Raw power. It is as if all of her Elemental abilities are intertwined, pushing their way through the tips of her fingers towards the blade.

As she looks up, a black fog races around the sword's edge, leaving a trail of darkness in its path. She screams, unable to remove her burning fingers from the handle.

Ruby woke up in her bed still screaming. She was covered in sweat and her eyes were trying to quickly adjust to the light coming in from the streetlamp outside. Rubbing them roughly, she opened them again to find Liam standing in the doorway.

"What happened? Are you all right?"

"I'm fine. Just a bad dream. Go back to bed, it's all right."

"I'll just lie down here if that's all right with you." He was already at the foot of the bed before she had a chance to answer.

They lay there in silence for what seemed like hours. Ruby tried to close her eyes, but sleep was not a friend of hers tonight. The dream had her mind in shambles. Even Liam's breathing could not lull her to submission. She hadn't felt that surge of power before, especially not in a dream. She could see the sword so clearly, and while no one had ever shown her any images of it, she knew that what she saw was the Sword of Enuma. There was something special about how it reacted to her in the dream, it was as if it had been waiting for her guidance.

She sat up abruptly in her bed. Suddenly clear headed and with a new realization of the dream's meaning. She knew exactly what she had to do in order to put a stop to the Elemental war that was beginning to bring danger to innocent bystanders. She had to somehow unite the four houses. It seemed the only way to do so was to gain control of the sword. It was waiting for her and she had to possess it.

"Liam?" she said and watched him sit up on the

floor next to her. "The dream I had, I think it was trying to tell me something."

"You understood one of your dreams? That's never happened before. What was it?"

"I saw the sword. In a room with walls dripping wet. I think I know who's holding it."

"Water house." He caught up fast.

"Exactly." Ruby did not go into the details of her plans for the sword, she knew that Liam's passion for gaining control of it would not coincide with her pacifistic plans. "I need you to train me."

"Train you how?"

"Everything you know. About combat."

"Look, whatever ideas you have, you can forget about them. You're not going to be with us when we finally make a play for the sword."

"You can't shelter me forever, Liam. If it's true that I have all four houses' powers, then I am your best bet at getting the sword. It also means that I am much stronger than you, so don't test me!"

"Ok, warrior." He smiled, "We can start training tomorrow. But if you're going to awaken all of your powers, you need to be prepared. This won't be easy."

"Nothing in the last few weeks has been easy. I'm ready."

CHAPTER 24
WALK TO THE RESISTANCE

The next week at the resistance was one of the most grueling weeks in Ruby's life thus far. Liam was not kidding when he said that it wouldn't be easy. She felt like she was part of an Elemental bootcamp.

Every morning started with physical exercise. She ran never-ending laps around the facility, switched to weight training, and ended with a half hour of meditation. Liam said the morning routine was the most important part of her training because powers or not, if someone physically attacked her, she'd have to know how to defend herself. The meditation was the only part Ruby actually enjoyed, but she couldn't deny the results; she was getting stronger daily.

After lunch, she spent an hour in the lobby going over old texts and trying to find out everything she could about the sword. Scouring pages of folklore and myth and separating fact from fiction in her notebooks, Zag often joined her for her studies since, outside of his time spent in the greenhouse, going over old texts was one of his favorite activities.

When her mind was tired from reading, Liam would pick her up, and they would make their way to the training rooms. Each day was assigned to a different Elemental house. Liam wanted to hone each of her powers separately so she could get a sense of how to control them better. Alice had actually recommended this approach based on Ruby's emotional triggers. Since Ruby needed to get certain emotions to come to the surface in order to access her powers, it was best to concentrate on one emotion at a time. She couldn't be certain, but she got the sense that they were afraid of what she could do if she combined her powers.

Their first attempt with this technique was with Fire powers. Liam wanted to start with something he knew inside and out in order to get the most out of the training session. They spent the day getting Ruby to feel angry, coaxing her to become a fire starter. They started with small pieces of paper again, but by the end of the day, if she was upset enough, Ruby was able to create flame out of thin air and even managed to throw a fireball at the wall next to Liam. He ducked out of the way so fast it made her laugh uncontrollably.

After Fire, came Water. The coffee trick Ruby

pulled in the library was cute but would be completely useless in a fight, unless she was battling it out for a latte. Unfortunately, the emotional trigger for her Water powers was sadness and while trying to create precipitation in a temperature-controlled training area, Ruby had gotten herself so upset that she started hyperventilating. Liam suggested they cut the day short, but she was determined to learn everything she could and stayed until almost midnight trying to start storms in a ten by ten room.

Air and Earth were a breeze to get through. Pulling oxygen out of a room was still not on the menu, but Ruby effortlessly manifested fog and wind and was even able to move large boulders a foot off the ground by tapping into Earth powers. Being happy and hopeful to get her powers to manifest was a much easier task, since Liam brought out both emotions effortlessly.

Ruby walked home every night that week with him by her side. He insisted on sleeping on the couch while Shaylah was still in the hospital, and she was happy to have him there. They watched movies each night until she fell asleep on Liam's shoulder, and every morning had coffee on the deck and listened to traffic dart by.

Their walk to the resistance was often filled with questions about each other. How they grew up, what their childhood was like, their favorite movies. Anyone watching would assume that they were a young couple on a date.

She could live this life forever.

But her small joys had an expiration date. Each day it all ended as soon as the pawn shop's doorway buzzed, and they made their way underground. With every step down, Ruby erased a portion of the night before and got ready for training. Every time her foot touched down on the floor of the resistance, she was no longer a girl getting to know a boy she just met. She was a fighter. A warrior without regard for her own life.

She was an Elemental.

CHAPTER 25

ALL OF IT

"You ready for today?" Liam asked, as they made their way towards the training room.

"I guess. I mean, the last time we tried Water I couldn't do all that much."

"Don't be so hard on yourself, I don't know what I would do if my powers depended on my emotions."

"Well, you're a guy, so you'd probably be powerless." She laughed, "Just kidding."

"Right." He was smiling, but she could tell she might have hurt him a little with her comment.

"So, what's the plan when we get in there?" she changed the subject.

"Alice said that since you'd had some success with the coffee cup, we should start there."

Ruby was still careful about what she said in front of Alice. She was sure there was something she was hiding, and until she found out what it was, trust wasn't on the menu. Despite her own feelings, she had to admit that when it came to Elemental powers, Alice was the one to talk to. If it wasn't for her, Ruby would never have figured out that her emotions ran the show.

When she walked into the training room, she almost tripped over. Liam had filled the entire room with about two dozen buckets of water. She looked at him in surprise.

"I may have upgraded the coffee cup." He smiled. "Oh! I have something for you!"

He reached into his pocket and pulled out a bright blue rock.

"Is that a sapphire?"

"Yup. I figured since the stones make our powers stronger, you could maybe use it to tap into yours."

"So, what do we do with these?" She gestured at the buckets, tucking the rock into her pocket.

"Same as always. Or have you forgotten it all already? Somehow, I thought you'd be smarter than this."

"Hey!" she yelled out, quickly realizing that he was trying to get her upset. "Just take it easy, we still don't know for sure that's going to work."

"Maybe this whole thing won't work. Maybe you being here is a mistake."

"Liam, stop."

"Stop what? You said you knew where the sword is

but as far as I can see, you're just some scared little girl playing with powers you don't understand. It's sad."

"I said, stop." This wasn't working. She wasn't getting sad and he was starting to cross the line.

"Why? You're scared you can't handle it? You need to remember your training."

"I do remember."

"Prove it. Your whole life you've been hiding behind a camera. You're scared of people, you can't talk to guys, no wonder your parents shipped you off to Westerlake." He saw tears start to form in her eyes. "Remember your training, Ruby. Or have you forgotten it like you've forgotten your friend in the hospital?"

He was wrong. This wasn't making her upset or sad. Nothing about this was going to help her move the water in the bucket at her feet. She didn't feel sadness, she felt everything, all of her emotions combined. They were coursing through her veins like they had been in her dream. Pushing through her system, looking for a way out. She could feel her emotions intertwine and form a ball in the pit of her stomach. Pulsating and sending energy to the tips of her fingers

"That's enough!" She yelled and pushed her hand towards him. The energy moved to the tip of her fingers and shot out in a black fog. It hit Liam's chest and catapulted him into the wall on the other end of the room. His back hit the metal, and he fell on the ground.

Ruby's eyes were wide with shock. She looked at her

hands, unable to believe what just happened. She bolted to Liam's side, tears still running down her cheeks.

"Liam! Oh my God!" She knelt beside him, cupping his face with her hands. "Liam, please wake up."

His eyes opened slowly, and he looked up at Ruby. Her tears were like waterfalls, and her hair a mess of loose waves across her face. He had never seen anyone more beautiful. He pushed himself up, so he was sitting in front of her. Her hands still on his face, he put his palm on the back of her head and pulled her in.

As their lips touched, Ruby's emotions settled. The ball in her stomach was gone, and she no longer felt like a ticking bomb of energy. She let him press her closer to him and felt the warmth of his lips transfer to hers. His hands squeezed her waist, pushing the air out of her lungs. Her temperature rose and her breath grew shallow. She pulled at his hair, using it to stabilize herself. Her body falling onto his hard chest, burning up from the heat rising from his skin. Nothing had ever made her feel like this. Powerful and weak at the same time.

When they pulled away, she studied his face as their thoughts shifted to what happened before the kiss.

"Well, that was new." he said.

"Which part?" Ruby smiled and put her hand on his.

"All of it."

CHAPTER 26
TOILETRIES

Ruby was frantically trying to squeeze the clothes she had tossed on her bed into an overnight bag. It didn't make sense to keep staying in the apartment. With Shaylah still gone and the amount of time she was spending training: she should be closer to the resistance. Even with Liam staying on the couch, she still felt scared in the apartment at night.

It wasn't tough to convince Liam to let her move in. They hadn't spoken about the kiss since it happened, but she could see he was ecstatic when she told him she was temporarily moving in. Maybe without the added pressure of worrying about her safety they could finally figure out what was starting to happen between them. Ruby was more than just confused about their relationship. She knew she wanted him, but that was about all she knew.

"How's it going in there?" he yelled out from the kitchen.

"It's ok. Just trying to figure out what I need to bring." She was narrowing down her outfit choices to functional attire.

"Well, don't stress over it. We can always come back and get what you're missing."

He was right. It's not like she was moving there forever. She eyed a dress she'd borrowed from Shaylah a few months ago and threw it in with the mix of sweats and jeans. She would probably never get a chance to wear it, but after the kiss, there was a new need in her to impress Liam.

You're being childish. It's not some cute vacation you're going on. You must concentrate on the plan.

It'd been days since her dream about the sword, and she still had not told Liam about her plan to unite the Elemental houses. In her defense, there wasn't much to tell. She knew she wanted to get a hold of the sword before any of the resistance Elementals had a chance to claim it. Especially Alice. If the sword got into the hands of the elders, there was little chance of ending the war.

She understood their need for its power. If someone was lording over her and her family for years, she would probably want the same. But that wouldn't stop a war. In fact, it would likely start a bigger one, Air and Water would not surrender without a fight. If the resistance gets the sword, she was certain the other houses would do everything they could to get it back. How many innocent people would be hurt in the crossfire? How many more humans would end up hospitalized like Shaylah?

She couldn't risk endangering more people. More importantly, if the visions she had about Jake were about his safety, he could very well be the next collateral damage.

The only thing Ruby could say for certain was that the sword had to end up in her hands, somehow. She still had no idea what she would do with it once it was found, but anything she did would be better than more fighting. Maybe she could get the houses to listen to reason, she had to at least try.

"I'm going to go grab a couple of coffees, you think you'll be done in fifteen minutes or so?" She peeked out through the bedroom door and saw Liam putting on his shoes. She wanted nothing more than to run over to him right now, to feel his burning lips on hers. But he'd been acting like that first kiss had never happened, and she was starting to wonder if he wasn't pretending. What if she imagined the entire thing? Worse, what if it was a vision? She was spending so much time daydreaming about the kiss that it never occurred to her to consider the possibility that her visions were getting stronger.

"Yeah, that should be fine. I just need to pack some toiletries."

She grabbed the dress from her bag and tossed it back in the closet. There was no time for her delusions of romance right now. Liam's casual behavior was how things had to stay between them for the moment. They both needed to concentrate on finding the sword and getting her in shape and ready for battle.

The broken camera lens on the table reminded her how simple life was before all of this. Before that awful train ride, before the Elementals, before her friends were in danger. But all of that was also before Liam, and if given the chance, she would not change a thing that happened. She needed him in her life.

Filling her bag with a few more things, she put on her boots just as the door handle turned.

"Ready?" Liam said from behind two giant coffee cups.

"As ready as I'll ever be." She smiled, and for the first time in a long while, she meant every word.

CHAPTER 27
WE NEED TO TALK

Her hands were on fire, but she couldn't feel the heat. There were embers in the corner of the room from the last fireball she'd tossed. Closing one of her fists, she let smoke escape from the dying flames.

One handed, she pushed a boulder from her side of the room to block the exit. Her other hand shot a fireball in front of it and the ground lit up in a blazing wall. She turned just in time to see Liam grab a knife from the table and lunge towards her. With both her hands intertwined, she pointed at the knife and shot a turbulent wind in its direction, knocking it out of Liam's hand and onto the floor.

Breathing heavily, she stood directly in front of him and flipped her palms. The air around them began to shift, forming a thick, black fog. She brought her hands together and sharply straightened her arm, pointing at the space between herself and Liam. The fog expanded and thickened, enveloping Liam. She could see him struggling to see through it.

She swiftly dropped to the ground and rolled towards the knife, grabbing it with one of her hands. One leg extended and still crouching she twisted like an ice-skater getting ready to leap, knocking the feet from under Liam. She pounced through the fog, landing seated on his chest. The knife at his throat. Game over.

"Ok, ok. You win." He was laughing and holding his arms up in defeat.

Ruby smiled and loosened the knife from his neck. She could see the red mark she'd left when she'd pressed into him and reached for his throat with her fingers to soothe it. Still sitting on top of him, she flipped her hair out of the way and began to lean in. She was almost an inch away from his face when she heard a clapping sound emerge from the other side of the fog still around them.

"Well done, Ruby!" Alice was standing only a few feet away from them. Each clap sent the fog away from her, revealing her face. She seemed pleased with Ruby's progress. "You've really picked up the training, I see."

Ruby brushed herself off as she got up to stand. She extended her arm to help Liam, who accepted without hesitation.

"I'm really impressed with you two. It seems that

Ruby will be a more integral use for the resistance than anyone could have expected."

"Alice," Ruby walked over to the elder, "any news on what that vision I had about Jake might mean?"

It had been weeks and no one had any new information. Alice had said she had tasked one of the elders who was proficient in symbology to decipher its meaning, but she hadn't heard anything since.

"We're still trying to figure it out. It wasn't much to go by, and since you haven't had another vision again, we're really flying blind here. But I promise you we will get to the bottom of it. Your friend will be fine."

"It's just, he's supposed to leave soon and..." she didn't know how to finish the sentence.

"You want to make sure you're around to protect him." Liam finished it for her. She could see the hurt in his eyes when he spoke about Jake. Maybe she didn't imagine their kiss after all.

"Well, yeah. He's my friend. I have to make sure he doesn't get caught up in this." She tried to reassure Liam with her eyes. "Like Shaylah."

"Don't worry, honey, we will figure it out. No one will let your friend get hurt." Alice put her hand on Ruby's shoulder. "For now, you should concentrate on getting stronger. You're no good to Jake if you leave yourself exposed to danger."

She turned around and walked out of the room, extinguishing the fires from Ruby's fireballs as she left.

Despite not trusting her entirely, Ruby was in awe of Alice. The way she carried herself and the ease with which she used her powers. She could only hope to be that skilled one day. Alice was right as always, she needed to practice. But how could she concentrate on honing her emotions with everything that was happening around her? She needed to have a clear mind in order to train properly and there was only one way to do that.

"Liam," She grabbed his hand and pulled him over to her, "we need to talk."

CHAPTER 28
SHAYLAH IS AWAKE

"What's wrong?" Liam's questioning eyes pierced through her, there was no turning back now.

"Nothing. It's not bad, I just..." What did she want to say here? "I just wanted to talk about what happened."

"Happened when? Right now? At training?"

"No. The other day, when we kissed."

"Oh. I mean, what's to talk about?" He shrugged and pulled away from her hand.

"Well, what did it mean?"

"Why did it have to mean something?"

"Uhm. I guess it didn't. I thought that maybe it meant something. To you." She felt foolish now. He obviously did not care, and she hadn't read the situation right and let herself get carried away. "Maybe I was wrong. Never mind."

He was already starting to gather up the props for the next training session. "All right. So, we're good?"

"I guess."

Ruby's cheeks looked like someone had painted her with freshly boiled beets. She was embarrassed, but even more than that, she was hurt. She cared for Liam, and she thought that what had happened meant that those feelings were returned. His reaction just now made her feel like a childish schoolgirl with a crush. There was nothing on his mind other than the resistance. How could she have misread the situation so badly?

She was about to walk out of the room to get some water from the kitchen when she saw her backpack move from the vibration of the phone inside.

"Hello? Yes, it's me." She nodded. "Of course! I'll be there shortly. Thank you for calling me!"

"Who was that?" Liam asked.

"The hospital. Shaylah is awake. She's asking to see me."

"All right, I'll just tidy up here and we'll head over."

"You know, it might be better if I go alone." Ruby wanted to get away from the resistance and from him. The last thing she needed right now was a reminder of the rejection.

"Are you sure?"

"Yeah. It's for the best, really. I think we both need a break from each other for an afternoon."

As she walked out of the room she looked back through the doorway. Hoping for some semblance of emotion, to give her a glimpse into his feelings for her. Anything to make her feel like she wasn't crazy and hadn't created an entire relationship out of thin air. Liam was crouched on the floor, cleaning up the mess from their battle. His attention on the training room.

Letting out a disappointed sigh, she ran towards the exit. Fleeing the resistance and her own broken heart.

CHAPTER 29
I CARE ABOUT YOU, RUE

Shaylah's face had begun to regain some color and Ruby was relieved to see her friend's rosy cheeks. She had crawled sheepishly into the hospital room while Shaylah's parents went to get some food, feeling an immense amount of guilt over her friend's accident.

"Hey, Fish. Thanks for coming." Shaylah said and started to sit up in her bed.

"Of course. How are you feeling?"

"Oh, you know. Like a house fell on me."

"I'm so sorry, Shay. I was so worried. We all were."

"It's not your fault. Wrong place, wrong time." Shaylah straightened the blanket on her to a more comfortable position. "Were a lot of people hurt?"

"A few. No one as bad as you."

"Lucky me, I guess."

Ruby's eyes were wells now, overflowing to the brim. The idea of her friend being in this situation made her sick to her stomach. She knew the attack wasn't her fault but still felt responsible. If she had just been more aggressive with the resistance maybe she could have found out about it before it was too late. What was the point of having all these powers if she couldn't even save her own friends?

"I really wish I could have gotten you out of there sooner."

"Yeah, about that..." Shaylah's questioning eyes watched Ruby in a hawk-like manner, "how exactly did you get me out?"

"What do you mean?"

"Well, I remember the building starting to fall apart, and being trapped under that giant marble block. Then you trying to lift it. I could have sworn you shattered it in half. Like, with your hands."

"What? You know I'm not some ninja, right?" She was trying to laugh it off and change the subject. "I probably kicked it in a weird spot when I was trying to move it."

"I know how heavy that thing was. There is no way you could have kicked it in half."

"Well, I don't know. Maybe it was already cracked or something. I'm honestly just glad that I was able to get the guard to help me."

"I guess. Yeah." Shaylah did not look convinced. "I

just think it's a little weird."

"I wouldn't worry about it right now; you need to concentrate on getting better."

"You should listen to her, you know." Jake said from the doorway. Ruby was so concerned with her friend that she hadn't even heard him come in. "You need to get some rest and get the heck out of this place."

"I know." Shaylah smiled. "Thanks for coming by guys. It's nice to see your faces again. Really."

Ruby squeezed her friend's hand and looked back at Jake. He was gesturing for them to leave. Shaylah needed to rest and get better. There was nothing either of them could do from inside a hospital room.

They were walking towards the subway when Jake stopped her in the middle of the street.

"Rue, we need to talk."

"Oh, ok. What's up?" Trying to figure out what he wanted to discuss.

"I heard you and Shay talking at the hospital. She has every right to be worried."

"What? Worried about what? Me?"

"Well, yeah. You haven't been acting like you, recently."

"I've just been stressed, that's all."

"You keep saying that, but I don't really think that's the case. You've been odd ever since you met that guy."

"Who? Liam?" So that's what this is about.

"I don't trust him. You need to be careful. Especially when he's around."

"Why? Jake, is there something you're not telling me? Because you're acting very weird."

"I just..." his face turned red, and he was nervously shuffling his feet, "I care about you, Rue. Not like a friend. I know we never talked about this, and I know you've been my friend since we were kids, but with everything that's been happening lately I just needed you to know. God, I feel stupid for even making you listen to this."

He managed to look up at her and smile. Her face was rigid, the wrong reaction but the only one she could muster at the moment. She had wanted to hear him say those words for so long, but now that it was finally happening, she couldn't picture a worse time to hear it. Between the Elementals and Liam, she no longer knew what she wanted. Did she still care for him the same way she had before meeting Liam? And even if she did, was she willing to risk his safety by getting closer to him now?

"I freaked you out, didn't I? I shouldn't have said anything. This is probably not a good time."

"No, it's ok." She grabbed his hand. "I'm just a little surprised."

He pulled away from her and started walking again. "Just pretend I didn't say anything. This was stupid."

"Jake! Please stop!" She ran after him and grabbed

him so abruptly that he spun on his heels to face her, not being able to bear another man turning her away today. "Please, don't just walk away. With everything that's just happened with Shay I've had no time to think about my own life. Or what I want."

"I know. I think I was just hoping for a different reaction here." She could see the disappointment coating his face like a thick layer of paint.

"And a few weeks ago, you would have gotten it. There's a lot going on right now. Do you think you can give me a little bit of time to think? Just to wrap my head around it all?" That was as much as she could say without going into the details of why she wanted the time. Even now, Ruby knew that her feelings for Liam would not diminish so quickly.

"Oh. Yeah, of course. Just, not too long." He teased.

"Wait! Aren't you leaving with your dad, like, any day?" She just realized that she'd been so preoccupied with the resistance that she'd completely forgotten to check in with him about the trip.

"Oh, that. It's on hold for now. There're some urgent things we need to take care of here first."

"Like what?"

"Just business stuff. Nothing fun. To be honest, after the incident at the bank, there's a lot to get through. We have a ton of meetings with building inspectors to find the root of the problem. It's been a nightmare."

"Do they know what happened there?"

"Not yet. They're saying it's the weirdest thing; the building was new and well maintained, so they have no idea how it could just disintegrate."

"Yeah, odd for sure." Ruby said playing along. Good thing no one was questioning how a podium could catch fire, or a five foot and some odd girl could break a boulder in half. "Hopefully, they can figure it out. I'm just glad that more people weren't hurt."

"I'm glad *you* weren't hurt." He brushed a piece of hair from her face.

Shay will get a kick out of this one. She thought.

They walked to the subway in silence, while Ruby's thoughts raced for miles on end. Just when she thought things couldn't get any more complicated, she had to confront her feelings for Jake. What would she tell Liam if she decided to give him a chance? Would he even care? The thought of him not caring made her stomach turn, there was no denying that their kiss meant a lot to her. A lot more than it seemed to matter to him.

She tried to laugh at the situation, only she could manage to fall into a love triangle in the middle of an Elemental war.

Jake got off the train a few stops before her, and despite his insistence on walking her home, she managed to get him to leave. She needed time to think, but her mind was preoccupied with the resistance. They were no closer to finding out where the sword was being held, and she still didn't know what she would have to do once they found it. She needed Liam's help, and the only way to get it was to fill him in on her plan to end the war. He wouldn't be happy about not taking control of the sword, but she was sure he would get on board once he heard her reasoning.

The announcement for her stop jarred her back to reality, and Ruby ran off the train, making her way to the resistance. Optimistic and full of hope.

CHAPTER 30
COCOON OF STORM

"Hey! I thought you weren't coming back for a while." Liam was sitting up at the edge of his bed when she finally made it back to the resistance.

"Yeah. I wasn't going to but there's something that's been really bothering me."

"About us?"

"No." She was done talking about them for a while. "About the sword. About this whole revolution you're planning actually."

"I don't understand. Why are you even giving it that much thought?"

"Are you serious? You literally pulled me into this whole thing to help you get the sword and now you're, what? Upset about the fact that I'm actually invested?"

"You're right. Sorry. I just don't know what else

there is to it. We get the sword. We take over the power, and we control Air and Water for a change."

"Don't you think that sounds like more of the exact same problem? More generations of kids growing up in hiding, unable to be themselves?"

"We're not like them. We don't want to control anyone; we just want the sword to level the playing field."

"But it won't be level. Don't you get that? Instead of them in charge, you'll be in charge. Someone is always left powerless."

"So, what do you suggest exactly? We live happily ever after?"

"Well, no. But kind of."

"What does that even mean, Ruby?" He was looking at her like she was possessed. Nothing she was saying made sense to him. He'd been set on the same goal for too long to see another solution.

"I might have a different plan for the sword. When we get it, that is."

"What plan, exactly?" He stood up, showing interest for the first time.

"I was thinking, since I can control all four house powers, maybe if I'm the one who holds onto the sword, we would have more leverage."

"No way. No."

"What? You're not even entertaining the possibility? Are you that dead set on having more power that you won't even try to do something with the sword that could benefit all four sides?"

"What would you know about it?" His anger came as a surprise. Liam was always the levelheaded one but something was different now. "You've been around us for all of ten minutes and think you're some savior that's going to swoop in and absolve us all? That's ridiculous!"

"I'm not saying I could save anyone! I'm just saying we should look at other options that won't result in more people getting hurt."

"And you honestly think that after this many years in power, Air and Water are just going to go along with some Kumbaya life where we all hold hands and live in peace? No offense, Ruby, but I thought you were smarter than that." His head shaking, he started walking away from her.

"First of all, you don't have to act this way or belittle me. Second of all, I am trying to help all of you and make sure that humans don't get caught in the crossfire. In case you've forgotten, I thought I was human just a short while ago, so I still have a lot at stake in their world."

"Well, right now, you're acting like one them. Clueless and childish. Training you was a mistake. You weren't cut out for this!" He stormed out of the room without another word.

She was hurt. Her eyes heavy with tears, not tears of sadness but of anger. How dare he speak to her this way? She deleted almost her entire life to help him with his mission and he wouldn't even entertain the possibility that she might be right? Is this really the man she thought she was falling in love with?

She fell heavily on the bed, grabbing hold of the blanket with both hands to steady herself. She was shaking. Her tear-stained face felt like it was on fire, and the anger she felt just a second ago turned into stultifying sadness. She was sobbing uncontrollably now, trying to control the shallow breaths in hopes that no one in the hallway could hear her. Around the bed, the air began to turn into wind, encircling her body in a cocoon of storm. She lay there paralyzed with grief as a tornado danced around her, knocking all of Liam's belongings out of place. Her Water abilities were leaving their mark.

CHAPTER 31
THEY'RE GOING TO DIE!

R uby opened her eyes just in time to see a book fall off the wall shelf above Liam's bed. She raised her arms defensively and managed to knock it out of the way.

"Oh crap!" She said, seeing the wind turbulence she'd created, and started to take deep breaths to calm herself down. The hurricane in the room subsided when Jenny, one of the older kids popped her head through the doorway.

"Ruby! We have to leave right now!"

She could see panic painting Jenny's face. "What's going on?" This couldn't be because of what just happened with her powers, could it?

"You didn't hear the alarm?"

"Huh? No..." She was embarrassed to admit that she

didn't hear anything over the sound of her own crying. Darting off the bed, she wiped her face and rushed towards Jenny. "What happened?"

"Something is going on. The elders must have set off the alarm. We have to get to the safe room. Now!"

Ruby started to run after her down the hall. Her mind clearer now, she heard the blazing cry of the alarm come into focus. There were other loud sounds all around. What was that? Screaming?

She slowed down and made a left turn at the atrium. She could hear more people in the cafeteria and rushed towards the voices, searching the halls as she ran. Despite their last conversation, she needed to find Liam.

The doors were closed. Ruby got closer to the windows and peeked in. There were four people huddled in the corner of the room. One of the Earth teachers was on the ground surrounded by three resistance members she hadn't seen before. It looked like they were trying to protect her from something, rubbing their palms together and attempting to make their powers kick in.

Ruby followed their gaze to the other end of the room where a tall, muscular man was holding out his hands and muttering something. He wasn't someone from Fire or Earth. Who was this imposter?

Her eyes searched the resistance members as they were struggling on the ground. Two had lost consciousness. The third, a girl about Ruby's age, was grasping at her throat.

He's Air! she thought, realizing that the room was being sucked free of oxygen.

Ruby reached for the door handle and was starting to push her way inside when Liam grabbed her by the shoulders, pulling her back into him. Holding her tightly as she tried to wiggle out.

"Let me go!" she yelled, "They're going to die!"

He didn't bother answering, instead grabbing her by the waist, he pulled her onto his shoulder and carried her away from the cafeteria. His speed picked up, dragging her along while she struggled. The halls were a blur, her vision zeroing in on small details to try and discern what was happening, but Liam was moving too fast. She could see resistance members running out of training rooms, some were staying back and getting ready for attack. As she looked back, she could see more outsiders coming down the hallway, using their foreign powers to attack the resistance members fighting back.

She wanted to stay and fight alongside them or at least to reason with the attackers but Liam's hold was too strong. He pulled open a door and threw her inside. Her body felt as if she had lost control of her legs. Tumbling forward, she tripped over someone's leg and fell hands first on the ground. She was on the floor of a room full of kids and members of the resistance. A large clunking sound turned her around to see Liam pull shut a barrel lock and use his hands to melt it shut.

We're in the safe room. She thought, as a large, rogue wave moved angrily outside, wiping the hall clear of people and debris.

Her eyes found Liam's, but even with him there, safety was far from reach.

CHAPTER 32
IT'S ALL DESTROYED

They got a signal from outside that it was safe to come out. Liam heated the lock until it could be pushed open from the outside and a few Fire resistance soldiers helped everyone out of the room. Ruby waited until all the kids were safely out and shakily made her way through the hallways.

The resistance had taken a big hit. Tables were turned over, walls were crumbled, and people's belongings were scattered everywhere.

She watched as the remaining soldiers covered bodies with tarps and carried them away from the common areas. It was hard to tell which house they belonged to, but Ruby mourned them all the same. Death was death in her eyes, no matter who it took.

As she walked, her eyes moved through the crowd to find Liam. She pushed past the crowds gathering around the training rooms and made her way towards the green-house. From the looks of it, the wave of water created by one of the attackers that she saw outside of the safe room found its way here. Zag was already cleaning up the mess inside.

"Zag!" She ran inside and hugged him. "I'm so glad you're ok!"

"It's all destroyed." His eyes were more than just sad, Ruby could see his heart was broken. "Everything we've created is gone."

"We can fix it. I'll help." She put her hand on his shoulder, "Have you seen Liam?"

"Yeah. He came by just before you, said he's going to his room to grab some things."

Her stomach turned, she needed to find Liam. She'd be back later to help Zag with the plants, but right now she wanted nothing more than to make sure Liam was all right. Knowing him, this was something he was taking personally, and who knew what he would do in return. He was packing some things into a bag when she got there. She made her way towards him and reached her arms around his waist. Turning his body to face her, he stayed still for a second and then pulled back. It was as if he wanted to hold her, but something was getting in the way.

"Looks like they did some damage in here, too." He said looking around the room. Ruby's cheeks reddened;

she knew the mess he was referring to was made by her when they were fighting.

"Right." She lied, "What the hell happened out there?"

"Isn't it obvious? Air and Water found our location. They were probably tracking us after what happened at the bank. We should have seen this coming. We should have been more prepared."

"How could you have possibly known?" She was right, he was blaming himself for what happened.

"Because it's what they do. They're killers, Ruby. That's all they are."

"I really don't think that's true."

"Even after all this?" He was pointing at the shattered glass in the hallway outside his room, "You still think you can reason with these people?"

"I have to believe that. Now more than ever." She moved closer to him and reached for his hand. "We have to do something to stop this war once and for all."

His hand jerked away. She could feel his anger as if it was her own. The heat was pulsating around him, and she knew he needed to calm down before the entire room was set ablaze.

"Liam, it'll be ok. We will figure it out."

"*We* will not be doing anything. You coming here was a mistake, and me pulling you into all of this was stupid and selfish."

"You don't mean that. You need my help."

"The only thing I need is for you to leave. I can't fight if I have to protect you all the time. We'll find the sword on our own. You need to go back home, Ruby."

"Are you serious?" she couldn't believe he was actually kicking her out when all she'd tried to do was help the resistance.

"Yes. It's not going to work out. Please leave."

There was no reasoning with him. She ran out of the room, holding back tears and pushing through people to get to her sleeping quarters. Once again, he had made her feel foolish for caring for him. When was she finally going to learn her lesson? He didn't want her. It was time for her to go.

Her head was spinning, and she leaned on the hallway wall for balance. Her mind was full of images. Visions as clear as the broken walls around her. Glowing marks, giant waves, Jake, and then suddenly her parents. Their faces aglow in the midst of the chaos. There was a darkness all around, but her father's hand was reaching towards her, pulling her to him. Her back pocket vibrated, jarring her eyes back into focus. Reaching for her phone she saw her family's number on the screen.

"Dad?" she said, still a little breathless.

"Ruby, honey, it's your mom. We heard about what happened at the bank. Why on earth wouldn't you call us?"

"I'm sorry, I just didn't want to worry you."

"You need to get out of the city, sweetie. Can you come stay with us for a few days?"

"I don't know..."

"Your father says it's not up for debate. We want you to come home right away." Her mother's tone was strict, and Ruby was certain that arguing was not going to help. If she were being honest, she was relieved to have a reason to leave for a few days. She needed to get away from the resistance, the Elementals, and most importantly, Liam.

"Sure, Mom. I'll catch the next train."

CHAPTER 33

THE FIRST-BORN AETHER

"O h, honey, come here!" Her mom greeted Ruby at the door with a massive hug, while her dad grabbed her bag. "I am so glad you're ok! We were so worried when we heard what had happened."

"Mom, it's totally fine. Shaylah was the one who got hurt. But she's ok now, so you don't have to worry."

"You know she'll always worry, right?" Her dad joked.

"Yeah, I know."

It was good to be home with them. Since she had gotten into Westerlake, she hadn't had as much time to visit them. They had always been a close-knit family and being an only child, Ruby knew how much they worried about her when she was away.

"Come, let's get some tea and catch up." Her mom

pulled her into the living room where she already had a few snacks out on the coffee table. "Hungry?"

"Always." Ruby said and pounced on the tiny sandwiches.

Her dad leaned on the couch next to her. His face was different, and she realized that there was worry coating every inch of it. "So really, Rue, how are you feeling?"

"I'm fine. What's going on? You guys aren't usually this worried." Something was off, she could feel it.

"It's just that..." Her mom was looking to her dad to help finish her sentence, "Dr. Olivian gave us a call a few weeks ago. She told us you've been asking about your grandma."

"Wait, what?" Looked like Dr. Olivian didn't care much for her privacy. Ruby was annoyed. "Isn't that supposed to be between her and me?"

"It is. She was just concerned, that's all."

"Rue, she said you asked her about symbols, and told her you were seeing things. Is that true?" Her dad interrupted.

"Uhm, I mean, it was." She didn't know how to start explaining everything else that started after. Seeing the symbols was just the start of it all. "There have been some other things."

"What things?" Her mom scooted closer to her on the couch.

"Just..." she said, not sure how to respond.

"Hun, you can tell us anything. You know that, right?"

"I know. But I'm warning you, it's going to sound a little crazy." She took another bite of her sandwich and started her story at the beginning.

"You guys don't look surprised." She said, when she was finished filling them in on what had been happening.

"I'm so sorry, honey!" Her mom hugged her again, "We were really hoping you wouldn't have to go through this."

"Hold on, what?" She pulled away, dumbfounded. "What do you mean 'hoping'? Why aren't you more shocked about this? I must sound crazy!"

"Well," Her dad said, and moved over to sit next to her. "I think it's time your mother and I told you about my family history."

"Jeffrey!" Her mom yelled out and slapped his shoulder.

"It's fine, honey. She has a right to know the truth."

"What truth, dad? What truth?"

"Our family is..." he took a deep breath in, "special. That's a good way to put it."

"Special how? Elemental special?" She said, feeling uneasy using the term in front of her parents.

"Sort of. That story of the sword that this Liam told you, well, it's all true but it's not complete."

"What?"

"The legend he told you has another part that might help explain things a little better for you." He looked back at her mom who was looking out the window, avoiding the conversation. "See, when the four house elders first forged the sword, they knew that no one house could be trusted to keep it. In order to keep it safe, they created a guardian for the sword. Someone made from one part of each one of the houses. The problem was that they were not powerful enough to create life. Not like the Gods who made them were."

Ruby was still shocked that her parents had any knowledge of the Elementals in the first place. "Ok..."

"They needed to combine their own powers with that of a deity, one that could control the Elements from another plane. The Elementals called upon the God of the Aether for help and consummated their powers with his to create a new being. A woman that was part Elemental and part deity. The first AetherBorn." He reached to hold her hand as if to prepare her for the rest. "For many years after, there was peace within the Elemental houses. But one day, the AetherBorn is said to have fallen in love. Out of that affair, a child was born. In order to keep the affair secret, the AetherBorn hid the child and raised the girl without interference from the elders."

"Why couldn't she just tell them? It seems brutal." Ruby said.

"The AetherBorn's only job was to keep the sword safe and to hold onto the peace between the houses. Being a mother, in the eyes of the Elementals, would be getting in the way of that."

"So, where are all these AetherBorns now, then? I haven't met one yet and I've met quite a few Elementals lately. Like a lot of them."

"Legend states that the royal son of the House of Air was also in love with the AetherBorn and that when he found out about the affair, he murdered her out of jealousy on her twenty-first birthday."

"But what about the baby?"

"Well, according to the story, the girl grew up orphaned, and mothered children of her own. Throughout the generations, the memory of the Aether-Born background was mostly forgotten. The Elementals continued their life amongst the humans, treating this part of their history as a myth, a fairytale to be told but not believed. But every girl born into the lineage gets a glimpse of the AetherBorns on their twenty-first birthday, when the sword calls to them. It provides them with the power of sight to guide them to the sword."

"My visions..." she whispered.

"Exactly. And your grandmother's."

"So, this whole time, you guys have been telling me that she was crazy, and lying to me about our past?"

Ruby looked at her mom who had been awfully quiet this entire time.

"Not lying, Hun." Her mom finally said. "We were hoping that this whole AetherBorn curse died with your grandmother."

"But you still knew all of this and hid it from me. It didn't occur to you to give me a heads-up or something? Like a 'hey, kid, just so you know, when you get older you might get some weird visions about a sword, so don't freak out when it happens!' What about when I have kids of my own? What would I tell them? That they're just imagining it?" She was starting to get angry with them and tried slowing down her breath to stay calm.

"We didn't want to fill your head with this stuff. Especially after what happened to your grandmother. The visions were too much for her to handle." Her dad's voice sounded sad every time he spoke of his mother. There was so much about her Ruby wished she could know. "Besides, it's not like this is something that my family advertised, I didn't even know anything about it until I was much older and found some of your grandma's journals in the attic. To be honest, it all sounded like nonsense to me at the time."

"Does Dr. Olivian know?"

"No, of course not. We just asked her to keep us posted in case you started asking about your grandma."

"You understand that if you'd told me about all of

this, I could have been prepared for it better, right? People got hurt! I could have stopped it!"

"Rue, please don't get upset." Her dad said. "Even if you knew about all of this, how could you have helped?"

"Besides, how were we to know you'd somehow stumble onto a secret Elemental resistance?" Her mom chimed in.

"Except, I didn't stumble into it. I was forced into it. By people who knew that I have visions. People who now want to hurt me and those I care about. For all I know, you guys are in danger, too! Liam never would have..."

She stopped mid-sentence. Who else knew about her AetherBorn blood? Was that the secret Alice and the elders had been keeping from her? Did Liam know about this, too? Is that why he agreed to train her?

Her head was spinning again, her entire life had been a lie. She was sick of feeling ill every time something happened. Sick of being weak, of needing protection and care. She didn't need any of them. She was angry. Angry and confused.

They've all been lying to me. She thought and the room went dark.

CHAPTER 34

MOVIE SELFIE!

"Jeffrey! Come here! She's awake!"

Ruby's mom was perched on the edge of her childhood bed when she came to. Her fingers clenched around a wet cloth that had left drips of water on Ruby's heated forehead.

"What happened?" She asked and tried to sit up.

"I'm not sure. You were sitting down and then you just lost consciousness. Sweetie you were burning up! I only managed to get the temperature down an hour ago, we were about to call the hospital."

Her dad's moccasins shuffled into the room, his face pale from concern. She was still upset with them, but her throat felt like a desert on a summer day, and she welcomed the glass of water in his hand without hesitation.

"We're sorry you got so upset. I told your father that we should have waited to tell you all of this until you settled in, but you know him, the patience of a hare."

She looked up at her dad, he always was quick to jump the gun. She remembered when she was little, her mom only had to mention needing something and dad would show up at the door with the thing in hand within hours. She always thought he was magical that way. Funny how the one thing she wished he was impulsive about telling her, somehow managed to become a dark, hidden secret.

"Look guys, I know you weren't actually trying to hurt me, but I'm not ok with any of it. You should have told me about our past and my connection to the Elementals. Hell, you should have told me about the Elementals!"

"Ruby Elizabeth Black!" Her mom scowled. "Don't you raise your voice at us. We were trying to protect you, and as far as I remember, we are the parents here."

"Sorry." She realized she was getting worked up and calmed down. "I really can't stay here right now, guys. I hope you can understand. I need to get back to the city."

"You expect us to just let you go back there with everything that's happening? Do you want to end up like Shaylah? Or worse?" Her dad moved to block the door.

"Dad, you can't keep me here. I just need to cool down. This is a lot to take in."

"It's all right, Jeffrey. Give her some space." Her mom said. "We're sorry you feel betrayed, sweetie."

"Mom, it's ok. Really. I'll come back soon. I need to figure this out for myself. What my life is now and how I want to live it."

She was surprised how understanding they were. With the way her dad was behaving, she half expected them to chain her to the bed and keep her tucked away from the world for the rest of her life. She wasn't sure if it was because they felt guilty for keeping secrets or because she saw them in a different light now, but her parents were no longer the giants she always imagined them to be. They were just human. Not AetherBorn like her, just two regular people trying to protect their daughter from dangers they knew very little about.

IT WAS ALREADY DARK out when she got back to the apartment. She had called Jake on the train ride back home to meet for dinner and a movie. As far as she was concerned, he was the only person in her life who hadn't been lying to her or keeping secrets. If Liam actually knew about her AetherBorn background like she suspected Alice did, then she couldn't trust him or anyone at the resistance. With Shaylah still in the hospital for the rest of the week, she wanted a normal night with someone who cared about her. Not because of a sword and not because she was some mystical creature.

She had just finished boiling pasta when she heard a knock on the door and saw Jake's face come into view in the hallway.

"Make yourself at home, I guess." She laughed, watching him kick off his shoes and plump down on the couch.

"When have I not?" He grinned. "What are we watching?"

She balanced the massive bowl of pasta on the coffee table and sat down next to him. It felt odd to spend time with him again, after their last conversation. She still had not given him an answer and tonight wasn't going to be the time to have that talk. "I don't know. You pick. I haven't even looked at what's out yet."

THEY SPENT the evening eating until they couldn't move and binge watching a new show Jake had found online. It was a comedy, and although Ruby was in no mood to laugh, the sound of Jake's boisterous howl made her giggle.

HOURS LATER, Jake fell asleep leaning awkwardly on a pillow. His one shoe off and his mouth slightly open. Sitting on the other end of the couch, she gaped at him smiling. Maybe it was time to forget about Liam? She'd been pining after Jake for so long and he was finally telling her everything she wanted to hear. What exactly was she waiting for here?

DISCREETLY GRASPING HER PHONE, Ruby stretched her arm out as long as she could make it.

MOVIE SELFIE! She whispered and took some rapid-fire photos.

THE MUSCLES in her stomach clenched as she scrolled through the images. There they were, two lovebirds on a couch. Just a normal couple on a regular night in. And it would have been, if it wasn't for the dozens of glowing inverted triangles covering Jake's skin.

RUBY'S HANDS shook as she started to understand what her vision really meant. This entire time that she'd been jumping through hoops and risking everything to save him, something else entirely was going on behind the scenes. She felt foolish but more than that, she felt betrayed.

• • •

JAKE WAS NEVER IN DANGER. He was a Water Elemental.

CHAPTER 35
I HAVE A PLAN

She was running down the street from the subway station. Her breath rapid and fast. She was more than human. A wildling escaping a predator, someone fleeing from danger at every turn. Her only thought was to get to the resistance and away from the truth she'd just uncovered.

When she finally managed to get rid of Jake without raising suspicion, the first thing she did was text Liam. Ever since one of the shop entrance guards got killed during the attack, no one came in or out of the resistance unescorted. It was like a secret treehouse club, no outsiders allowed.

She waited by the pawn shop doors trying to wipe the sweat off her forehead when the bell finally rang behind her.

"I thought you were staying at your parents for a

bit?" Liam said, as she was already pushing past him to get downstairs.

"We need to talk."

"All right. Hello to you, too, I guess."

There was no time for pleasantries right now. "Sorry. Hello. We need to talk."

They made their way to his sleeping quarters. She could see a lot of work had been done in the short while she'd been away. The resistance was starting to look a little more like the place she remembered. With the addition of guards at every entrance and a few extra locks on the doors. His own room had been tidied up quite a bit. If she didn't know better, she never would have guessed that just a short while ago she had completely destroyed it with her powers.

"So, what's going on that couldn't wait until morning?" Liam sat on the chair by his desk and let her take the bed. She sat down cautiously; the last time she was in this bed she nearly broke all of his belongings with a hurricane.

"Jake is Water House."

"Hold on, what? How do you know? Are you sure?"

"I saw the marks on him. And yes, I'm very sure."

"This is..." He didn't know how to react, "surprising."

"It's not surprising, Liam. It's goddamn garbage! He's been an Elemental this entire time and I had no clue!"

"Do you think he's the one who gave out our location?"

"Well, I do now!" She was baffled she hadn't thought of it before. It made sense. If he ever followed her, he would figure it out sooner or later. "I just... I don't know what to do right now."

He walked towards her, and she could feel her heartbeat quicken as he sat on the bed next to her. His hand found hers. The tension in her shoulders dropped and she sank into the bed defeated. How had she let her life become such a mess?

"We will figure it out. I promise. I know this is a blow. I'm pretty shocked myself, to be honest."

He couldn't understand. It wasn't shock she felt right now. It was trauma and distress. She felt victimized, lied to, taken advantage of. All of the things friends are supposed to protect you from. Her friend, someone she considered family, betrayed her in the most unimaginable way.

"I feel like everyone has been lying to me. Jake, my parents, you..."

"Me?"

"I know about the AetherBorns, Liam. You can drop the act." As much as she didn't want to, she pulled her hand away from his to make a point. "My parents told me everything."

"Oh."

"That's it? Oh? You and Alice, and I don't even

know who else, have been keeping this away from me the entire time and all you can say is 'oh'?"

"We weren't keeping things away from you. Well, I guess we were. But I asked Alice not to say anything to you until we were sure."

"Sure, about what? How to use me for your little plan to get the sword?"

"How to keep you safe, Ruby. I don't want Air and Water finding out what you are and making a play for you.".

"A play for me? What does that even mean?" She yelled.

"I'm assuming your parents told you about the AetherBorns connection to the sword?"

"Just that the girls in our family are like guardians of it or something."

"It's so much more than that, Ruby. You don't just guard the sword; your kind was created to use the sword as a way of controlling the Elementals. Whatever power Air and Water had so far by mere possession of the sword would be amplified by a million with you around. They could wipe the rest of us out in seconds if they wanted to." He reached for her hand again, "Well, you could anyway."

She looked at his face, he wasn't kidding. He really believed she was in danger of being taken. Of being controlled. Ruby had no idea how someone could force her to do something she didn't want to do, but after everything she had seen lately, she erred on the side of caution and believed him. She still didn't know how to feel about him after he rejected her but when it came to this, she felt that she could trust him to have her best interest at heart. "But why didn't you just tell me?"

"Because I knew you'd want to be some hero and try to save everyone if you knew what you're capable of. I thought that if we didn't tell you who you were, you would just stay out of it and help us from a safe distance. But, of course, you had to go and come up with your little plan for the sword, anyway."

SHE THOUGHT back to their fight, when she told him about her plan for the sword. It all made sense now. He was trying to protect her by getting her to leave. She wanted to lean over and kiss him. To tell him that she understood why he did it. That she forgave him. His face was flushed and when he reached over to brush the hair out of her eyes, she turned the same shade of crimson.

"EVERYTHING I'VE DONE SO FAR WAS to protect you." He said.

. . .

"I KNOW." She jumped up from the bed rapidly. "That's it!"

"WHAT'S IT?"

"I KNOW how to get the sword! Get the others, I have a plan."

CHAPTER 36

SHE'S MOST CERTAINLY NOT
GOING IN ALONE

Liam had gathered a few people in one of the meeting rooms. They stood around the round table and watched Ruby's every move. She guessed that everyone here knew she was an Aether-Born. Zag and his sister Leah stood closer to her and Liam, while the elders huddled together at the opposite end, led by Alice. They were much older but held the same strong demeanor as Alice, forming a unified front of Elementals, all awaiting Ruby's words. This was her first time meeting the Earth elders, and she couldn't help but study their faces. They were afraid. Whether of her or of what was coming, she wasn't sure.

There were two Fire soldiers guarding the door, and Liam assured her they could be trusted. Ruby did not want any ears in the room that he couldn't vouch for. This plan was too important.

"What's this about, Ruby?" Alice said.

"I know where the sword is, and I have a plan on how to get it. But before we go through with this, I need everyone to understand that the sword goes to me first. No one is to touch it."

"Sweetheart, I understand you've been through a lot, but I don't think you're equipped to handle this. We have people who have been training for generations for this day, let's let them make the decisions here." Alice's voice was condescending, but Ruby let it slide. She had had enough, there was no more time to play by their rules.

"I didn't come here for opinions, Alice. I am an Aether-Born and the sword belongs with me." She could see Alice's eyes widen. Liam hadn't told her that she knew about her family. Talking back like this to Alice felt wrong but she needed them to take her seriously. She wasn't going to just sit back and wait for someone else to get hurt by their dumb war. Shaylah could have died in that attack. What if next time she's not so lucky? "You're either with me in this fight, or I go alone. But I sure as hell will not stand by and watch another pointless battle. Not when I can prevent it."

"All right." One of the Earth elders pushed past Alice and stepped up to the table. His wrinkled hand landing on the table to expose dirt ridden nails. He looked back at his twin sister as he spoke, her face as wrinkled as his hands, nodding for him to continue.

"And how do we know for sure that you know its location?"

"Turns out, I've known where it is this entire time. The sword put itself in my path so that I could find it." She turned her eyes to Liam. "This all would have been a lot easier if I'd known who I was when I first found out about my powers."

"I agree." Alice said. Maybe she had an ally in the elders after all.

"The sword is with the Water house. If we're going by sheer power, I'm willing to bet it's being held by Cyril Okenos."

"Cyril is a Water Elemental?" Zag piped in. "I honestly would have thought the mayor would have it, being Air and all."

"She probably did." Ruby said, "But after the attack in the bank, I'm certain it was moved. Cyril is methodical, he always has been. Leaving the sword exposed would never be an option."

"Where would he move it to?"

"Cyril's offices. I'm sure it's there. As close to him as possible."

"How do you even know he's Water? This seems far-fetched." Zag was looking at Liam for support, but Liam's eyes were on Ruby.

"Because his son, Jake, is Water. I saw the marks."

"Sorry, Ruby. I didn't know. That totally sucks." He

patted her on the back in support, but she shook it off. She was done feeling sorry for herself.

"Look, my best friend is an Elemental. Does that suck? Yes. But it gives us an in. I can use my connection to him." She looked around the room at everyone's confused faces.

"How exactly?" Alice asked.

"He cares about me. A lot." From the corner of her eye she saw Liam's face grimace. "And he's waiting to hear if I feel the same way. It sounds trivial now, I know, but it's the perfect way to get close to the sword. I'll have to tell him what I am. Pretend I want to be with him..."

"I don't like it." Liam interrupted, and she smiled. It was nice to see him jealous.

"Tell him I can help him and his family, act like I want to be on their side." She continued as if Liam had not spoken. "Once he takes me to the sword, I can make a move for it and get out before anyone figures out what happened."

"Sorry, so, you're planning to go into the Air and Water den alone and trick them into leading you to the sword? Absolutely not. No way. Too dangerous." Liam pushed his balled fists onto the table to prove his point.

"It's our only shot, Liam. No one else could get close to the sword like I can. Nobody would even know where to look!"

"Alice, are you hearing this?" He said.

"I am. And I don't like it. But it's the only way in. Ruby is right."

"What? You're planning to send her out there by herself without any protection at all?" He was shouting now, and Ruby rubbed his hand to calm him down.

"I didn't say that. She's right in that she's our only way to the sword, but she's most certainly not going in alone."

"You don't think I can handle Jake?"

"It's not Jake I'm worried about, sweetheart." Alice walked over to Ruby. "You'll need back up in case things get out of hand."

"Ok. But how?"

"Well, we know the location. Liam and the team will be nearby, waiting until you find out where they're keeping the sword. Once you have the details, they will follow you into the building as backup. Just in case something goes wrong."

"I don't want anyone else to die, Alice."

"I understand, Ruby. But we need to make sure you don't either."

She looked around the table. There was no arguing with them now. If Ruby wanted to get her hands on the sword, she would have to work with them. The idea of Liam coming with her left her helpless. What if something happened to him? What if the plan didn't work and he got hurt?

The stakes were too high for her now. She had to

help the resistance get the sword, it was the only way to stop the bloodshed. Their entire future depended on Ruby convincing Jake that she loved him.

Better get to practicing your lines. She thought and leaned on Liam's shoulder.

CHAPTER 37

ONCE AND FOR ALL

R uby watched Jake pick up their coffees from the counter. She was nervous about what was coming next, she hated lying, even if it was to someone who had betrayed her. Elemental or not, she couldn't erase their past friendship overnight. She saw her phone vibrate on the table and threw it in her bag, convinced that it was Liam checking in.

"Just milk, right?" Jake pushed a coffee cup towards her.

"Yeah! Thanks!"

"So, what's up?"

"Oh. Right." She took a deep breath in, time to get it over with. "I wanted to talk about what you said the other day."

"Finally." He smiled, "I thought I freaked you out."

"I mean, kind of. Just caught me off guard, I guess."

"Sorry. I really don't want to pressure you. I know you have a lot going on right now."

"More than you know..." she said, hoping to start getting to the point.

"With school, you mean?" He was playing dumb and she knew it.

"I know what you are, Jake. Please stop pretending."

"What I am?"

"Seriously, drop the act. If we're going to be together, we can't have secrets. And being an Elemental is kind of a big secret to keep, don't you think?"

His face was stern but not surprised. She could see his lips turn upward; he was grinning. Like he was happy she was calling him out. "Be together?" He said.

"Well, yes. Unless you changed your mind..." This entire plan depended on Jake wanting to be with her, if he changed his mind, the resistance was in big trouble.

"No, of course not! I'm just surprised, that's all." He reached over and grabbed her hand. It took her everything not to jump back. "I'm really happy, Rue."

She stared at his face, trying to find things wrong with it. Evil, hateful things to make her despise him for what he did. For being involved with the Elementals that had hurt so many of her friends. But all she saw was the boy she grew up with, the boy who, up until very recently, she had wanted nothing more than to be with forever.

"Me, too."

They spent the rest of the afternoon catching up. Jake was surprised to hear how much she knew about the Elementals. She told him about the resistance, leaving out Liam and a few other parts that could make him question her motives. He, in exchange, filled her in on his involvement with his father's business. Turns out, that he wasn't just next in line for the business, he was being groomed to be the head of house, upon Cyril's retirement next year. Evan's death had hit the family hard, he was the stronger of the two brothers and Jake stepping in meant his entire life was derailed.

"Can I ask you a question?" Jake was nervously playing with the spoon in his coffee.

"Sure."

"Why did you take so long to answer?"

"Honestly?" she said, "When I found out about the Elementals, I wasn't sure I wanted you to be involved. I'm sure you can imagine how I felt. You've known about this your entire life, imagine finding all of this out right now? No warning at all, just thrown in the middle of it on a regular afternoon?"

"Yeah, I can see how that wouldn't go over well."

"Well, that's an understatement. When you told me how you felt, I literally didn't know how to react. Then, when I found out who you were..."

"How exactly did you find that out, by the way?" He interrupted.

"Uhm, here's the thing," It was time to tell him about her part in all of it. "I kind of can see Elementals."

"See them how?"

"I get these visions. I can see things that other people can't. Oh, and powers! I kind of have a lot of those."

"So, you're..." She could see him piecing it all together.

"An AetherBorn? Yep. Looks like it."

"How did you even find this out? You had no idea before?"

"Not a clue. It just kind of fell in my lap and, well, here we are." Ruby knew it was time to kick it into high gear, Liam was probably anxious to hear back from her with next steps. "Hey, Jake?"

"Yeah?"

"Remember that night we went for food and you had to go back to your dad's office?"

"Uhm, yeah. Why?"

"Well, my place was broken into. By Elementals. Any chance your dad had something to do with it?"

"Rue, I'm so sorry." His face sheepish, looking down, unable to make eye contact. "My dad was convinced you were a threat somehow. I swear, I had no idea about the whole AetherBorn thing or what he was planning. He just said we needed to make sure the resistance backed off. He kept talking about Evan and how we needed to pay them back. I can't..."

"Wait, what? What about Evan?"

"The accident, Rue. It wasn't just a coincidence. You know Evan, he would never sail the boat into land. Those rocks were put in his way. My dad is convinced it was an Earth move. Nothing I say matters to him when it comes to my brother's death. I tried to stop it, I swear, I..."

"It's ok. I'm not mad." She lied. She was as mad as she could be. How could he think that it was alright to break into her home like that? Whether he was right about his brother's death or not, she could never forgive him for letting his dad treat her that way. "But I need him to know I'm not a threat. In fact, I can help him. After what the resistance did at the bank, after Shaylah, they need to be stopped. I can help all of you with handling them."

"What? How?"

"I need you to take me to him. I need to speak with him and the mayor right away. We might not have much time."

"Time for what, Rue?"

"To silence the resistance once and for all."

CHAPTER 38
I WILL NEED TO SEE THE SWORD

The elevator ride to the top floor of the Okenos office building was faster than Ruby anticipated. Being the tallest building in Westerlake, she half expected a scenic ride to the top, like you'd see in tourist attractions, but they reached the top floor within seconds.

She had managed to sneak away to the bathroom before they left the coffee shop to text Liam. Her instructions were to distract the elders while the resistance broke into the building as backup. Once they were in position, she was to text again and wait for their attack before making a move for the sword. It looked good on paper but having seen one too many bank robbing movies, Ruby wondered how well the plan was actually going to play out.

"Ready?" Jake asked, and squeezed her hand.

"Can't wait." She forced a smile on her face, hiding her nerves and fear.

The elevator doors opened to reveal a large, open space. There were windows on either side of them and looking out made Ruby nauseous. Long way to go if things don't work out.

This floor was different than any office building Ruby had seen before. It looked more like a lab than a financial institution. The hallway walls were all frosted glass and she could see people in white coats in some of the rooms.

"Most of the research on Elementals and their powers gets done here." Jake stated, seeing her confusion about the space.

"Research?"

"Where we practice our abilities, study literature, and..." he thought carefully about his next word, "store artifacts."

The sword! She thought. She was right about its location.

"Got it."

They walked to the last office on the floor. It was housed behind two massive metal doors with Elemental markings carved into it. This place was very different from the resistance, which right now felt more like a dungeon than a training ground.

"What's with the marks?" she asked.

"Protection symbols. They're supposed to enhance the power in the room. At least that's what my dad says."

There were two guards standing on either side of the office entrance, Ruby could see their Air symbols glowing from down the hallway. Her powers of sight were getting stronger now, she was sure the sword had to be nearby. The guards would prove to be problematic if the plan derailed even slightly, hopefully, Liam was expecting some opposition and was coming prepared. Jake nodded in approval and they stepped aside to let them pass.

"Hey, dad! Someone wants to see you!" Opening the door let a blinding amount of light into the hallway, the office was surrounded by windows.

When her eyes adjusted, Ruby could see that Cyril was not alone. Next to his desk stood Elena Vanti, in her usual heels and fashion-forward suit.

That explains the guards, she thought. *The mayor's watch dogs.*

She was so mesmerized by Elena's appearance that she almost didn't notice that Rhea was also in the room, sitting on the couch opposite the desk, entertaining Mihaela and Ioana. Ruby wondered if Jake's mom's entire job was to babysit the mayor's children.

"Hello, Ruby." Cyril said, "Rhea, darling, do you mind taking the girls for a walk?"

Rhea got up without so much as a protest and shuffled the kids out of the room. She could see Elena wink at her girls as they walked off and was relieved to know there was a heart behind the stilettos.

"Hi, Mr. Okenos. Ms. Vanti." She nodded in their direction.

"Oh, please!" the mayor exclaimed, "Elena and Cyril will do just fine."

"Ok." Ruby said awkwardly. She was not about to start getting friendly with them.

"Jake mentioned you wanted to talk? That you have some information about the resistance that would be of use to us?"

Her eyes widened, it seemed small talk was not on the menu for today. It shouldn't have come as a surprise, everyone in the room was already aware of her powers and what she was, but it was still jarring for Ruby to speak about it so openly. Especially with people she barely knew. The most time she'd spent with Jake's parents while growing up were a few awkward dinners, and this was her first time actually speaking to the mayor. If she wasn't so motivated to get to the sword, she would have been star struck by their presence.

"Not information." She said, getting back to the plan.

"Oh?" Elena was intrigued.

"Me. I am what will be of use to you." Ruby straightened her back, her mother always said that good posture exuded confidence and that is exactly what she needed right now.

"I see. How exactly?"

"I think we can all stop the charades here." She walked over to the window, trying to see if she could spot resistance members outside, but they were too high up. "I am an AetherBorn, no need pretending otherwise."

She looked back at Cyril and the mayor. They were speechless. No condescending remarks, she had them hooked.

"I am assuming the Sword of Enuma is here? That is the 'artifact' you were alluding to?" she asked Jake, who was a minute short of hiding in the corner of the room. She felt bad, giving out information would likely not go over well with Cyril.

"Yes, you're correct." Cyril said, eyeing his son like a sniper. "What does that have to do with the resistance?"

"Well, they want it, of course. Or did you think the attack on the bank was their big performance?"

"It did seem odd, them laying low after we..." Elena stopped talking.

"What? Found where they operate out of and killed a bunch of people?" She was starting to get upset. "They're getting close to figuring out where the sword is and when they do, you'll have a war on your hands."

"And how exactly do you propose we stop them?"

"You don't." She said sharply. "I do."

The room was quiet enough to hear the heartbeat of each person in it. No one spoke a word and she could have sworn Jake was trying not to breathe, just to stay quiet. The time had come to close the deal.

"Having the sword might have been useful this far, but these are not the same times as those of your ancestors. Fire and Earth want to come out of hiding, they are pissed, and they want to take over. Your possession of the sword will not help. They have the numbers and they are ready for a fight."

"I'm still not sure where you come in." Jake said. She could see he didn't like how involved she wanted to be.

"I am an AetherBorn, Jake! My ancestors were literally created to wield and guard the sword. I am the only one in this room who can bring it to its full power, and if you're smart, you'll use that power to continue your dominance over the other Elementals."

"You'll have to excuse my son, Ruby. I'm sure you can imagine how shocking this is for us to hear. How do we know we can trust you?"

"You can't. All you can be sure of is that the resistance put my best friend in the hospital. They have no control and more innocent people will be hurt unless we stop them." She hated using Shaylah as a bargaining chip, but what she was about to say next was not any better. "You can trust that I love your son and I want to help him. Oh, and I'm assuming you'd like to prevent the deaths of humans and your own houses, right?"

They fell silent again. Cyril did not look convinced,

but Elena walked in front of him and stood by Ruby. She put her hand on her shoulder, and Ruby could feel the weight of the power it carried. Like she was in the presence of royalty. "Well, where do we start, then?" she smiled.

"The sword." Ruby said and pulled away from the mayor. "I will need to see the sword."

CHAPTER 39
UNDERWHELMING

There was still no response from Liam since her last text to him. She had no choice but to follow through with the plan and trust that the resistance had her back. As she followed Jake down the corridor, her stomach turned with each step.

"We're here." Jake said, breaking the deafening silence.

Her hand pushed open the door in front of them and she felt a chill from the metal. Her palms tingled, feeling the sword was within reach.

The room was dark, with just a few pot lights shedding streams of light around the perimeter. Ruby had expected a grander entrance but instead, she found herself in a space that resembled a library wing of a museum. There were books filling the shelves on the wall opposite her and a single desk and chair in the corner. The other three walls were adorned by large, antique gold frames surrounding abstract works of art.

"Well, this is..."

"Underwhelming?" Jake said and smiled.

He walked to one of the paintings and lifted the frame from the wall, setting it aside to reveal a hidden safe. The safe door was covered in symbols similar to those in Cyril's office, which seemed foolish to Ruby. The sword didn't need their protection, the only guardian it needed was her. She tried to see the code Jake entered to unlock the door, but he was too far away from her to catch all the numbers. The safe swung open, causing a light to flicker on a piece of metal inside; the outline of the sword resting on a satin display case.

Ruby walked slowly towards it, her eyes studying the weapon. It was simple in design and if not for the stones adorning its handle, she would have thought it was just a show piece. Like the fake swords she'd seen in party stores while looking for a Halloween costume. The golden handle was tarnished, with decorative carvings barely visible in their antiquated state. There were five stones cast into simple settings. Ruby did the math; the ruby, emerald, sapphire and diamond were all representative of the four houses. What was the onyx at the top for? She gazed at Jake for answers, but he looked disinterested, like he was showing her his mother's fine china collection.

Her hands started to heat up the closer she got, and

her vision flickered between blurred and razor focused. Ruby felt like someone was pointing a flashlight in her face and pushed the palm of her hand in front of her eyes.

"Are you ok?" Jake asked. He rushed towards her and caught her by the waist right as she was about to collapse.

"Yeah. Sorry. I just got a little dizzy." She steadied herself quickly and shook her head.

She needed him out of the way. This was her only shot to grab the sword and get out of there. She couldn't wait to text Liam for a rendezvous point in the building. There was no way she wanted to be stuck in this place alone with the sword in tow.

Squeezing Jake's arm tightly she pulled herself up to stand, seeing the worry on his face pushed daggers of guilt into her. Despite everything, he did really care for her and she hated what she had to do to him in order to go through with the plan.

I'm sorry. She thought and pulled him in for a kiss.

His lips were cold at first and he seemed hesitant to kiss her back. She tightened her grip on him, taking control of the situation. She was balancing on her toes to reach his lips, her hands pushing against his chest. His arms wrapped around her waist, and she could feel him press her tightly towards him. A part of her still wanted this to be real.

Light bounced off the sword and she remembered

why she was there. Her hands fell to her side and she closed her eyes tightly. A black fog formed at the base of her feet and slowly enveloped the two of them. She pulled its energy inward, breathing it in and directing it towards her hands. She could see Jake open his eyes and begin to pull away from her, fearful. Her hands cupped together, she pushed them to his chest abruptly and watched as the darkness shot him across the room, making him slide across the floor, and land face down, unconscious.

There was no time to think now. She ran towards the safe, trailing black fog behind her with each leap. Her hand reached for the sword and as she grabbed the handle, the stones on its handle pulsated light. She could feel the weight of it in her hand, lifting the weapon to study it. The fog danced around her arm, making the Sword of Enuma look as if it was surrounded by a black fire.

Behind her, the doors swung open and she twisted around to face the intruders. Cyril and Elena stood in the entrance, calm and collected.

"Now, let's not do anything foolish, darling." Cyril grinned.

He stepped aside and Ruby watched two soldiers enter the room holding Liam and Zag at gunpoint.

"Put the sword down or your friends die."

CHAPTER 40
WE AREN'T MONSTERS

"Don't do it, Ruby!" Liam shouted. The guard who was holding him dug the gun deeper into his forehead and she could see him wince from the pain.

They'd caught him. They'd caught him and he was going to die if she didn't make a decision soon.

Ruby looked around the room. She was panicking and breathless, but she knew she had to get herself together. If they were going to survive this, she had to gather her thoughts and find a loophole. Fast.

There was no way to escape, this she knew for sure. They were surrounded, and she would have to make a choice. It was either saving his life or helping the resistance. She knew what he'd pick if the tables were reversed. But she wasn't him, she wasn't anything like him, and for the first time it seemed like that might actually work in her favor.

Out of the corner of her eye she could see his lips moving. He was mad. Likely yelling at her to run, to leave him behind. She couldn't worry about his feelings right now. She knew what she had to do. Her hand gripped the sword's handle tighter. Her breath steady and calm as she gathered her strength and prepared for what came next.

I choose how this ends. Not them.

"Ruby, honey, we don't want to hurt anyone." Elena made one step towards her. "But you don't really think we are going to let you walk out of here with the sword, do you?"

"Let them go!" She screamed.

"Look, Ruby. We aren't monsters. We will let you all go, but you need to put the sword down. Now."

She looked at Liam and Zag, they were in no shape to fight their way out of this. If they had been captured, and from the looks of it beaten, the rest of the resistance was probably facing the same fate. There was no way they were going to walk out of here alive if she didn't do something quick.

"They're lying! You know they're lying!" Liam was struggling to get free.

"I'm not going to let them kill you!" She felt her eyes fill with tears.

Liam's eyes met hers, apologetic for what he was

going to do next. His hands pressed against the guard who was holding him, burning through his shirt until he collapsed. He moved quickly towards Elena, shooting a stream of fire towards her. Her screams cut through the room, bringing Ruby to the ground. She could feel the burning pain coming from the mayor.

Using the sword for balance she pushed herself up, scanning the room for Liam. She could see him in front of her, but something was wrong. His eyes were emptying of life, the green in them becoming dull and distant. His hands fell lifelessly to his side. From behind him, Cyril grinned, dropping a blood-covered knife to the ground. The metal hit the floor, followed by Liam's body. Blood stained the marble around him, inching closer to Cyril's shoes.

"Liam!" she screamed and started to run towards him but her eyes caught Cyril's gaze. She knew if she moved any closer, she and Zeg would suffer the same fate.

Ruby closed her eyes. She wanted nothing more than to hold him right now. To be back in the training room, his fiery lips on hers, pulling her closer and making her feel safe. She thought about her parents, watching her mom cook dinner while her dad told his terrible jokes. Her mind raced over her life, like snap shots in a photo album. Going to school, watching movies with Jake, Shaylah in the hospital.

Her hand gripped the handle tighter. The room

started to spin, and she dug her feet into the floor for balance. Ruby raced through time, going back through everything that happened since that incident on the subway. The air around her began to move with her thoughts, to shift as if it was moving up and down at the same time. She tried to focus on Liam, but his face was starting to blur. Ruby felt like she was watching everything in the room through a carnival mirror, a bystander to her own life.

The room filled with black, dense fog. She tried to push her hand through it, but it was thicker than a wall. The only thing still visible was the onyx on the sword, glowing like an LED lamp on steroids. Her emotions seemed to rush to the surface, running under her skin like a million ants, looking for a way out. Her stomach turned from the movement of images around her. *What the hell is happening?*

She squeezed her eyes shut to contain the vertigo that overcame her. Her mind started to slow down. An image of Liam in front of her. His eyes, lips, hands. She studied them intently, trying to remember every detail. Refusing to accept the fact that he was really gone. Breathing slowly, her hand let go of the sword handle. She waited for it to hit the ground, but the room was silent.

Ruby opened her eyes. A light danced from number to number on the panel in front of her. She was in the elevator with Jake again. The sword was nowhere to be seen.

She glanced at her watch; four thirty-seven. It was as if the last hour hadn't even happened. Ruby was scared. Was she losing her mind? Did she actually get to the sword? Was Liam captured?

"Ready?" Jake said, as the elevator door opened.

She looked around and saw the openness of the Air and Water research facility. They were back in Cyril's office building, making their way to his office. Ruby followed Jake to the marked, metal doors and watched as the two guards moved aside to let them pass. She'd been here before, in this exact moment.

"Hey, dad! Someone wants to see you!" she heard Jake yell out.

Holy crap. She thought. *I travelled back in time.*

CHAPTER 41
DO WE HAVE A DEAL?

"Jake mentioned you wanted to talk?" Elena said.

Ruby waited until Rhea and the girls were out of the room to start talking. She remembered this all too well and knew exactly what Elena would say next. There was no time for chit chat. The original plan wouldn't work, it would only lead to more death. To Liam's death.

"Actually, I didn't come here to talk." She said. "As we speak, resistance members have already broken into the building."

"I'm sorry but why..."

"Why am I telling you this?"

She studied their startled faces. They didn't believe her but that was fine. She would make them believe. She threw her phone to Jake who jumped back in surprise but still managed to catch it.

"Read out loud the last message I sent."

"I'm in, the sword is on the top floor. Will text with location once I have it." Jake's eyes shot up at hers, confused and demanding an explanation.

"You can call your guys downstairs, but trust me, no one will answer." She said as Cyril put the phone in his hand down on the table. "The guards are either incapacitated or worse."

"Ruby, why are you telling us this? You understand the position you're putting yourself in, correct?" Elena walked to the couch and sat down. Trying to look relaxed, to hide the fear in her eyes. The fear one feels when they have been blindsided. She had them trapped with her words.

Her eyes shifted to Cyril, wanting nothing more than to end him. She could feel her anger rushing to the surface and took a deep breath to calm down. "Trust me. I understand everything all too well."

"So why?" Jake said.

"I'm here to make a trade."

"I'm sorry?" Cyril was intrigued.

"I have something that you need. I'm here to trade for it."

"And what exactly do you have that could benefit us?" Elena was grinning, not realizing she was playing right into Ruby's hands.

"Me. You can have me."

The room went silent. She could hear the leather of

the couch move as Elena leaned in closer. Cyril sat down on the chair at his desk and was watching her without blinking. She had their attention.

"You have the power. You have the sword. And now you can have an AetherBorn. I will go with you willingly without a fight and will stay as long as you wish. I can help you use the sword."

"And why do we need that?"

"Because we both know that you want this war to end as much as I do. You said it yourself, you're not monsters." She said, catching Cyril look at Elena in confusion.

Oh, right. They haven't said that yet. She thought.

"And what exactly do *you* get out of all of this?"

"You don't harm the resistance and you let me call them off and leave here peacefully. They will be led by a Fire Elemental. I want your word that nothing will happen to him."

Jake's smile dropped, realizing that she'd used him, that she had no intention of being with him. She hated that she'd hurt him this way, but there was no other option. Liam's life was in the balance.

"So, do we have a deal?"

Cyril turned to Elena who nodded in agreement. He picked up the phone and whispered something into the receiver. A moment later, the doors opened and one of the guards from outside walked in. He started to make his way to Ruby, but she put her hand up in front of him.

"I want to hear you say it." She said.

"You have a deal, Ruby. We will not hurt them; you can call them off." He looked at Jake who reluctantly walked over to Ruby with her phone.

She texted Liam and handed the phone back to Jake, watching as he walked away from her. She tried to find his eyes, but he turned around and looked blankly out the window, his hands balled up into fists.

Well, that was easy. She thought as the guard pulled her arms behind her back and tightened the cuffs.

CHAPTER 42
AN ANIMAL ON DISPLAY

Ruby's back was straining. She'd been sitting on the floor of the glass room for a few hours now. The concrete was cold against her legs and she felt like an animal on display. She wondered what this room was used for before it was an Aether-Born cage. Maybe a meeting room.

THE GUARD STATIONED outside of the cage left a while back and Ruby wondered if he was coming back soon. He wasn't much of a conversationalist, but it would have been nice to have at least some contact with the outside world. She guessed, since there was no risk of her escaping, it might be a while before she had any visitors.

· · ·

RUBY STRETCHED her legs and knocked on one of the glass walls. The sound echoed around her. She wondered if Cyril and Elena had kept up their end of the bargain, or if Liam was being held in a cage much like this one. Her mind was still with Liam when Jake walked towards her.

"I THOUGHT YOU MIGHT BE THIRSTY." He opened a latch on the clear door and handed her a glass of water.

IF SHE REALLY WANTED TO, she could probably do some damage right now, but she had other plans.

"THANKS." She said, taking a giant sip. "I'm glad you're here."

"COOL. So, what the hell was that, Rue?"

SHE COULD SEE he did not want to be there. Right or not, she had really hurt him. Ruby tried to imagine how she would feel if the tables were reversed, and it was him who toyed with her emotions instead, but all she could think of was Liam. "I'm sorry. I really didn't mean to involve you in this. I care about..."

"Let's not." He interrupted. "I think you've done enough talking about us for today."

This was it. She thought. *No going back to being friends again.*

"Jake, I really am sorry. But this is bigger than me and you. It's the only way to stop this war. I had to do everything I could, please understand that."

"Well, you got yourself locked up in a cage, so no, I don't get it at all. How exactly is this helping anyone?"

"I know how this looks." She rubbed her wrists on the spot where the handcuffs used to be. This all must seem very strange to him.

"I just don't get what happened, Rue. One minute you're telling me you want to be with me and the next I'm watching you get cuffed. What was your plan exactly? What could you even do from in here? This room is power proofed, there's no getting out."

"I'm not planning to get out."

"So, what the hell are you planning, exactly?" He raised his voice, despite all she did, he still wanted to save her.

"I need your help."

"Oh, this should be good." His eyes widened.

"Jake, come on. You know as well as I do that your dad and Elena are never going to let the resistance live this down."

"Why do you care about them so much? It just doesn't make sense. I would have thought after everything; you would have been on our side."

"There are no sides. Don't you get it? As long as the houses keep picking sides, there will always be war. The resistance will always want to take over and your houses will never let go of their control. If it continues, you'll all fight until you wipe each other out entirely. And who knows how many others in the process." She remembered Shaylah's pale face in the hospital that day. "How many more people have to get hurt before you realize that there is another way?"

"Even if you're right, I don't know how I can help you. You're in a cage!" He punched the glass with his fist without causing so much as a crack.

"Look, I didn't just get myself locked up here for fun. I've seen how this plays out already, and it doesn't matter who takes control of the sword, it will end in death."

"Seen how this plays out?" He asked.

"How much do you know about AetherBorns? What they can do, I mean."

"I don't know, Rue. There hasn't been one in generations. All I know is what my parents told me. That they're more powerful than any Elemental house and that the last AetherBorn died quite young. But that's all anyone knows, there aren't too many texts on this stuff, as you can imagine."

"Well, that sucks." She said, hoping he might know how she was able to move through time.

"Yeah, you're kind of a big surprise to everyone."

"I gathered that much. That's why I think I might be the only one who can unite the houses again. I have to at least try."

"So, what are you planning on doing exactly?"

"Well, I have an idea, but you're not going to like it. If it doesn't work, I might be in more trouble than I already am."

"Ok..." He said, ready to hear her plan.

"Oh, and there's something else..."

"What's that?"

"You'll have to work with Liam. It's the only way this is going to work."

She could see he wasn't happy about it. his face was getting red with anger. There was no time to worry about Jake's feelings right now. If this was going to work, she needed both him and Liam to follow her instructions. She moved closer to the air holes in the glass, walking him through the plan before the guard made his return.

There was no turning back now.

CHAPTER 43
I THINK I'LL LET RUE EXPLAIN

Jake held her tightly by the arm as they walked down the hallway back to Cyril's office. He had followed through with the first part of her plan and arranged for all the house elders to meet straight away.

Cyril was not inclined to agree to the meeting unless the stakes were high, and Ruby had convinced Jake to leverage her life in exchange for the meeting. As far as Air and Water were concerned, the meeting was put in place for her execution. Jake had managed to persuade his father that a dead AetherBorn was worth more than a live one and that Ruby's execution was the only thing that could put Earth and Fire in their place. Even though she had managed to save Liam, she knew Cyril's bloodthirst for holding onto his power would cloud his judgment. He'd do anything to keep Fire and Earth under his thumb.

She was initially quite certain that her plan to unite the houses would prevent her own death, but walking towards the office now, doubt was clouding her judgement. If she could not sway the elders, she had no doubt Cyril would murder her just to prove a point. She looked at Jake for reassurance, but his stare was rigid. He was playing the part of her guard down to a T.

Jake pulled harder on her arm as they walked through the metal doors. She could see Cyril and Elena perched side by side at the desk. To her right, Alice and Liam stood by the couch. His eyes stalked Ruby, checking to make sure there was not a bruise on her. She could see smoke coming off him, he was furious. Behind them, sitting across from one another were Myriam and Harvey. The twin Earth elders made her smile. Their polite and calm demeanor calmed her nerves, and she needed to stay calm in this moment more than ever.

She stumbled to the center of the room, making sure to position herself directly in front of Liam. The sword had already been brought in and was resting comfortably on the desk next to Cyril.

Planning on offing me with it for effect, I see. She smiled. He was playing directly into her hands.

"Thank you for joining us, Ruby." Elena waved at her, eager to start the proceedings.

"Didn't have much of a choice, did I?" She said and moved a little closer to the sword.

There was no time left to waste. She started coughing, pressing her hand to her throat. Holding her breath for as long as she could, her face turned a deep shade of red. She punched at her chest and continued coughing.

"Get her water!" Jake yelled at one of the guards who scurried out of the room immediately.

Ruby dropped to the ground, her hands still at her throat. From the corner of her eye she could see Jake look at Liam and nod. Within seconds, Liam was running towards the guard positioned at the door. He raised his hands, shooting a fireball into his chest and jumped forward as the guard's body slid across the floor. Landing in a crouch he slid a knife from his boot and held it tightly under the guard's neck.

Her eyes shifted to the desk, Jake was standing behind Cyril and Elena. His arms outstretched in between two guards with a gun pointed at each of them.

"Jake, what is the meaning of this?" Cyril said, pushing his palms together.

"Please, don't do it, Cyril. No one has to get hurt here." She said, and watched his hands float back down to his lap.

Ruby slowly walked over the to the sword. Elena started to get up as she reached for the handle, but she could see Cyril pull her back down. The door behind her opened and she swung around, sword in hand, as a stream of black fog shot from her hand. The guard she hit fell to the ground and she cringed as the glass of water he was holding shattered next to him.

"Ruby, darling.would you please explain what's happening here?" Alice said.

"Well, you're here for my execution, Alice." She saw Liam's head spin around towards her.

"Jake. I need you to start talking. Now. This is not what we discussed." Cyril's face was determined, not being in control did not sit well with him.

"Sorry, dad. I think I'll let Rue explain."

The room was silent, and she could hear her own rapid breath. Her palm pressed tightly on the sword's handle. She dragged its edge across the floor, forming a light scratch in the marble. The stones on the sword's handle brightened, and she could see the blade begin to smoke.

"Actually, how about I just show you instead?" she said and lifted the sword's point above her head releasing a wave of black fog into the room. Like the remnants of an atomic bomb marking its territory.

CHAPTER 44
ANSWERS IN HER EYES

Ruby had no idea if her plan would work or not. Even if she was able to draw on the sword's power to see the future, she would still need to project enough of her own power in order to communicate the vision to the elders. Her initial plan was rooted mainly in assumption and hope that her connection to the sword was as strong as she had seen in her visions.

As the fog covered the room, she could feel the sword's energy burn into her hand. Her thoughts were scattered, and she had to concentrate to keep her mind on the visions. She could see bits and pieces start to come together. Blood, killing, and bodies of human bystanders filled the streets. There were glimpses of Elementals fighting in broad daylight, some were using their powers while others were shooting opposite house members in the streets. Every vision of the future she saw included bloodshed. Children cowering behind their mothers in buildings set ablaze.

When she was sure she had a full grasp of the future, Ruby pointed the sword at Alice. Much like in her dream, the ruby on the handle glowed brighter. She could feel herself tap into Alice's mind, directing the vision towards her. Tears flooded her eyes as she watched the vision manifest itself in front of her. The training center was burned to a crisp, not a sign of life in it. The vision shifted, moving up the steps towards the back entrance to the pawn shop and out into the street. A street covered in the bodies of Fire and Earth Elementals that managed to escape the fire only to be slaughtered at the exit.

Her arm struggled to move the weight of the sword towards Myriam and Harvey, their hands clutched each other's in a shaking embrace. What she saw in her mind was almost the same image of the two of them. Huddled together in their quarters, holding hands. Their bodies charred to a crisp. There was a wall of rocks on either side of them as if they had tried to shield themselves from the flames by using their powers. But they were either too late or not strong enough.

Ruby buried herself deeper into the visions, extending her arm to Elena. She traced her face with the sword, connecting to her most cherished possession and showing her what will become of it. She could see the terror on Elena's face as she watched her daughters cowering in her office covered in blood. Elena's blood.

By the time she made her way around, she was shaking from the weight of the metal.

As the sword's point landed on Cyril, Ruby moved her thoughts to Jake. She saw him on the floor of the resistance, struggling to create a tornado with no success. The spurts of wind he pushed from his hands lasted for mere seconds and very soon, he was not able to use his powers at all. His abdomen was bleeding from a previous attack, and he was crawling backwards, away from someone he feared. Ruby's vision shifted to his opponent and she watched as Liam's fired up hands shot towards him. The fireball hit his chest and his body folded forward and hit the ground. Jake's breathing slowed to a stop and within seconds, he was dead.

"That's enough!" Cyril shouted.

The shock of his words sent shivers down Ruby's arm and she dropped the sword. The fog lightened and disappeared. She looked around the room at the elders and the impact of her visions. Their faces were pale and there was something different about how they watched her, like they were looking for answers in her eyes.

Cyril walked over to Jake and whispered something in his ear. He glanced reluctantly at Ruby and lowered his aim on the guards who immediately made their way towards her. She already knew where this was heading and did not fight as they tightened the cuffs.

He walked out of the room grabbing the sword as he went, followed by the other four elders. Ruby smiled as they left, her visions were enough to convince them to talk. That would have to suffice for now.

CHAPTER 45
THIS IS IT

It was a few hours until the elders finally returned. The adrenaline Ruby had felt before had worn out, and she had a throbbing headache and pain running up and down her arms. She could feel the weight of the sword even though it was no longer with her and wondered how much she'd underestimated their bond.

The door creaked open and the guards that were keeping a close eye on Liam and Jake stepped aside to let the elders through. Ruby attempted to read their expressions but not one of them was making eye contact. She was losing hope quickly, eager to hear what they had to say.

They shuffled back into the room, taking the same spots they were in prior to their departure. Cyril put the sword down on the table and walked towards Ruby.

Flashes of the image of Liam's limp body ran through her mind making her blood boil with anger when she looked at him. He nodded at one of the guards behind her who quickly walked towards them. Liam's back straightened, ready to fight if needed.

This is it. She thought. *I'm dead.*

She closed her eyes as the guard came closer, unwilling to witness her own doomed fate. Within seconds, there was a click at her back and the handcuffs fell to the ground, leaving an echo as the metal hit the marble.

"You should probably take a seat. I would imagine this has been a tiring evening." Cyril smiled and gestured at the couch.

"I don't understand," she said, looking around at the other elders, "have you made a decision?"

"We have." Alice reached over and hugged her. "Surprisingly, we have."

"How much do you know about this..." Elena treaded carefully, "disagreement between our houses, Ruby?"

"Uhm, just what I've been told by the resistance. Some from what I've read in the old books. So, not much, I guess."

"Sadly, that is almost just as much as the rest of us." Elena looked back at Cyril; his gaze fixed on the sword. "Our two houses have been in control of the sword for so long, that entire generations grew up protecting it. Holding on to its power like a golden goose."

"I'm sure you can imagine, that when someone wants to take away the one thing that you have known to be true for thousands of years, you will do everything in your power to stop them." Cyril's eyes were on Ruby now.

She understood that very well. She had been fighting to hold onto the life she knew before the Elementals this entire time. What she didn't understand was what any of this had to do with their decision. All she wanted was to know if they had reached an agreement or if she had failed.

"We were taught from a very young age that this is how power is divided. That if our houses hold the sword, the Elemental race remains safe and secure. That we were preventing a war by following in the footsteps of our ancestors." He glanced at Myriam and Harvey. "What we had failed to see, was what that meant for the other houses."

"The war our ancestors were trying to prevent is exactly the one we ourselves have started." Alice said.

"So, what now?" She asked. The room went silent. Cyril touched the Onyx on the sword and jerked his hand away immediately.

"You are what happens now, Ruby." He looked at her and for the first time she saw kindness in his eyes. "You let us see what our actions were amounting to, the world we would eventually destroy. The people who would..."

Cyril stopped; his eyes were on Jake.

"I guess the human side of us was too blind to see the consequences." Alice continued for him.

"And now?" She asked. "What happens now that you know?"

"Well, we came to understand one very important thing." Elena walked over to her, placing her hands on Ruby's shoulders. She could feel the cold air moving around her, Ruby was more in tune with the elders than she had been before, more affected by their powers. "As long as any of our houses hold the sword, we will always end up in the same place. Generations will come after us and will fight for the sword and for their freedom. Sooner or later, our kind will destroy each other."

"And take the humans with you." Ruby added.

"Precisely. That is exactly what we must avoid."

"But how? No offense, this is all great to hear, but how, exactly, do you plan on changing that? You said it yourself, there will always be a war." Liam piped in but was shushed by Alice.

"It's quite simple, you see. We were so busy protecting the sword we never thought about something as fundamental as sharing it."

"Sharing it?" Ruby asked. "You can't exactly work out visitation rights here."

"No." Cyril laughed. The sound felt unnatural to

Ruby, likely because this was the first time in years that she had heard it. "But we can make sure that each house holds a piece of it so that the full power of the sword is never united unless we all agree to it."

She took a step back. If this worked, it was actually a pretty good plan.

"Wait, what's to stop someone from just killing all of you and putting the sword back together?"

"Well, there is a catch." Alice said.

"Ok..."

"It's been a very long time since there was an AetherBorn guarding the sword. None of us can actually break the sword and we definitely can't put it back together. Only you can do that."

"What? I wouldn't even know where to start to do that."

"It's all right, Ruby. We will be with you to help guide your powers. Although your connection to the sword is unlike anything we've ever seen before."

"We know this is a lot to take on. We're asking you to become..."

"Like a queen, or something?" Jake yelled out from the corner of the room. He had been so quiet that she almost forgot he was there.

"More like a guardian. But if you prefer, I'm sure we could get on board with queen." Myriam said and smiled. Her toothless grin put Ruby at ease immediately.

"You can take some time to think about it if you need." Cyril said.

"No. I'll do it."

Her mind was racing. She wasn't sure what she was getting herself into, but at this point, if it meant the houses were in unison, she had to go along with it. She would do anything to stop this war, even if it meant spending the rest of her life in their world. A world of powers and demi-Gods and... Her thoughts landed on Liam.

She turned around and looked at the spot where he was, only to find it empty. She panicked. How had he managed to slip away? She was so entwined in her thoughts she hadn't seen him walk out. She was about to run out of the room and chase after him when she felt a tap on her shoulder.

"Looking for me?" Liam said, as she swung around towards him.

"Always." She smiled.

She wanted to talk to him about what just happened. To over analyze everything the elders said and have him tell her it would all be all right. But more than that, she wanted to kiss him one more time. Her hands reached for the back of his head and she jumped up to hug him. As his arms wrapped around her waist, she could feel the rest of the room disappear. He was the only thing that mattered now. She felt his hard chest against hers and leaned in closer. Their lips met and she breathed in the heat he was surrendering, cooling it down within her own mouth. They pulled away, suddenly realizing the room was still full of people.

"So, how about you let me take you out on a real date?" He said.

"Sure," she smiled. "But I get to pick the place."

"Whatever you say, my queen." he laughed, and squeezed her hand.

She couldn't believe it. Her plan had actually worked. Ruby looked at the sword and heaviness filled her body. For the first time, it wasn't the sword's power that she was feeling. The weight she was experiencing was burden. The burden of being responsible for the lives of all Elementals, the burden of controlling the peace. Trying to smile, she walked to the sword, running her finger across the blade.

So, this is what it feels like to be an AetherBorn.

CHAPTER 46
JUST GOING FOR PIZZA

Ruby watched Shaylah dump dress after dress onto her bed. She was pulling everything out of her own closet and holding it up to Ruby's face before throwing it onto the pile. She was happy to have her friend back to normal again but could definitely do with a little less enthusiasm. It seemed that Shaylah was more excited about her date than she was.

"How about this one?" she asked and pulled up a leopard print mini.

"Definitely not." Ruby said, cringing. "Shay, this is super casual. We're just going for pizza."

"I know, but the way you talk about this guy, it has to be perfect! How about this one?"

"That's a hard no on that one. Didn't you wear that to your cousin's wedding last year?"

"Oh, yeah. And they're divorced now, so, probably not a good choice. Bad juju."

Ruby laughed. She was really hoping to wear her usual tee, ripped jeans and sneakers, but it seemed her friend had alternate ideas. After spending much too long analyzing everything Ruby owned, they settled on a simple black dress and nude pumps.

"So, have your parents met him, yet?"

"Uhm, not yet. But probably soon."

"You mean, when they move down here, and you have no choice?"

"Yep. Pretty much."

When her parents found out what happened with the elders, and the choice Ruby had made to be the sword's guardian, they were adamant on being closer to her. She could have sworn her dad was putting the house up for sale before she'd even hung up the phone. Selfishly, she was glad they would be closer, but a big part of her wanted them to stay away. Not just so she could ensure their safety but also to have her own privacy. There was so much about her life now that she needed to figure out. It was as if she were learning how to live all over again, this time as someone other than human.

Looking back at her friend as she ran out the door, she wished she could share this new journey with her. There were so many things she wanted to get her opinion on. The elders, her role as a leader, dating an

Elemental. But she knew that the more Shaylah knew about that world, the more danger she was in. Besides, the rule of 'no powers' in front of humans kind of meant she had to keep secrets.

"You sure you want to wear that thing?" Shaylah asked, pointing at the enormous Onyx stone hanging from Ruby's neck. The only piece of the sword she inherited in the division.

"Yes, Shay. I already told you, it was a gift and I like it."

"Fine, but don't you dare change into those flats in your purse when you leave!" Shaylah yelled out the door as she ran downstairs. "They do nothing for the outfit!"

THE NIGHT WAS WARMER than usual, and she got whiffs of different foods as they walked past the shops on the street. They had eaten almost two whole pizzas at the restaurant, and Ruby suggested they walk back to her apartment to walk it off. The idea seemed quite romantic when she said it, but now her feet were throbbing, and she wanted nothing more than to get into her leggings and watch a movie on the couch.

"You look beautiful tonight, you know." Liam said.

"Thanks." She reached into her purse and pulled out the pair of flats. "Do you mind if I get just a little bit shorter?"

Liam's laughter filled the street and she started to laugh with him. If Shaylah was here, she would slap her. She tried to hold onto his arm for balance but he grabbed her waist and pulled her in close. Their eyes met, and she started to pull in closer to his lips.

"Uhm... Sorry to interrupt."

Ruby jumped back, startled to see Zag standing in the middle of the sidewalk watching them.

"Zag? What are you doing here, man?" Liam asked. She was wondering the same thing.

"I know it's timing, but it couldn't wait. You'd better come to the training grounds quick."

"What's wrong, Zag?" She asked, feeling for the Onyx necklace.

"We have a big problem."

CHAPTER 47
SOMETHING WE'VE NEVER SEEN
BEFORE

The familiar walk to the pawn shop was quicker than usual. They almost ran to the resistance, now known as Elemental Training Grounds, without exchanging so much as a glance. This was definitely not the date she was hoping for.

"Zag, what's going on? What happened, exactly?" Liam was getting upset with the lack of information, and she reached for his hand to calm him down.

"Let's just get downstairs, I'll let Jake tell you."

As they made their way down the stairs, Ruby realized the extremity of the situation. If Jake was willing to interrupt their date, something must be really wrong. They had not spoken about what happened since the elder meeting, and Ruby had no intention of bringing it up. All she wanted was to have her friend back, but she

265

knew he needed time away from her. She'd hurt him when she chose Liam; she'd hurt herself as well. Jake was all she'd wanted for most of her adult life, and now the comfort of his presence was almost non-existent.

"Hey, Jake. What happened?" Liam reached out his hand to shake Jake's as they walked into one of the training rooms. "Zag made it sound like the world was ending."

"Well, he's not totally wrong." Jake was looking at Ruby now, his eyes searching for guidance from her. She felt the Onyx start to burn into her skin.

The sword! She thought.

"Is it the sword? What happened?"

"My father's piece. It's gone. Someone took it."

"What do you mean gone? Isn't it more guarded than the Louvre?" Liam exclaimed.

"It is. That's why we don't know how it happened. No one had access to it except the elders and Ruby. It's like it just... disappeared." There was discomfort in his voice, he wasn't happy having to speak to Liam and it showed in every word.

"Things don't just disappear, Jake." She said. "People take them. I need to get to Cyril's office. Now."

She ran out of the room and made her way back outside. Her feet were moving quickly now, despite having not had a chance to change out of the heels. How could this have happened? Who could have taken the sword piece? And were they coming after the rest of the pieces next?

RUBY LED the way out of the elevator with Liam, Jake, and Zag on her heels. She walked straight towards the end of the hall to the room where the Water sword piece was kept. The two guards stationed outside the door stood up straight when they saw her, and she wondered why they were still there. There was no sword piece left to protect.

"Evening, Miss Black!" One of them said and stepped aside to let her enter. He could not have been much older than Ruby but was already strapped with two guns and a bullet proof vest.

Ruby ran into the room, throwing a smile in the guard's direction as she entered. There was no evidence of a break in. The books on the shelves were undisturbed and the painting on the wall hung perfectly in place. She took it off and placed it on the floor next to her. Liam started to rush over to help but she waved him off. This was AetherBorn business now.

The lock was untouched and much like the rest of the room, spotless. She placed her palm on the sensor and listened for the locking mechanism to respond to her touch. A second later, the safe door slid open revealing the empty display case that used to house the sword piece.

The Onyx vibrated at her neck. She clutched at it with one hand and used the other to circle the room. Black fog moved from her palm to fill every inch around her. She moved quicker and with every turn, the room got darker until she could not see a foot if front of her. Her eyes opened and a cold wind pushed from her palms to clear the fog. As the blackness dissipated, glowing black marks appeared on the walls around them. Her mouth gaped open. The marks were every-where. They covered every part of the walls, ceiling and floor. She could hear their energy scream within her.

Ruby looked from wall to wall, memorizing the shapes. Running to the corner desk, she grabbed a piece of paper and frantically drew what she saw. Every line, circle and symbol.

"Guys?" she said, "Have you ever seen anything like this?"

"Uhm, Ruby?" Liam said quietly, "You might want to get out of this room now."

"Why? What's wrong?"

"These aren't Elemental marks."

"So, that means that whoever took the sword..." she whispered.

"Was something we've never seen before."

She looked up at Liam, his eyes were wide with wonder and fear. Her fingers laced around his as the symbols faded from the walls around them. The weight of the Onyx on her neck felt almost as heavy as the weight of the Elemental world on her shoulders. Her grip tightened and she sighed in relief. Whatever was coming next, she was glad she didn't have to face it alone.

THANKS FOR READING!

I would love it if you could leave a short review of the book to let me know what you thought. You can post your review at any of the sites below and I hope you know how much I appreciate you doing this!

https://www.amazon.com/dp/B07NY3HFHF

https://www.goodreads.com/book/show/44091935-aetherborn

If you want to hear more about my books or be the first to receive news on sales and giveaways, sign up for the newsletter!

https://www.ansage.ca/newsletter-1

A.N. SAGE

AETHERQUEEN

THE AETHERBORN SAGA, BOOK 2

AETHERQUEEN, BOOK 2 OF THE AETHERBORN SAGA

What good is a queen if she can't protect her people?

When Ruby Black was dragged into the centre of a war between powerful Elemental Houses, she faced a fight for survival with her very life on the line. Now, the war is over; shattering the Sword of Enuma into fragments and bestowing them equally among the Houses, Ruby herself was the architect of that peace. More than that though, she is Queen, elected and protected by the Elemental deities she once feared.

But peace is a fragile thing, and when the sword fragments begin vanishing from under the noses of the Great Houses, the threat of war looms once more. The pieces must be found, but with the only clue being a series of cryptic symbols found at the scene of each theft, she'll need all the help she can get.

Dark forces are moving in the shadows, and they threaten to bring all she has worked for crashing down.

If a queen cannot rule, chaos will reign in her place.

BUY ON AMAZON NOW!

https://www.amazon.com/dp/B07QMW1ZVD

ALSO BY A. N. SAGE

Kartgega- Kartega Chronicles Book 1

https://amzn.to/2YFSekp

Kartgega 2.0: A Star Reborn- Kartega Chronicles Book 2

https://amzn.to/2ZhT7yR

AetherQueen- AetherBorn Saga Book 2

https://amzn.to/38mMGyJ

AetherBlood- AetherBorn Saga Book 3

https://amzn.to/2VuUxov

AetherWars- AetherBorn Saga Book 4

https://amzn.to/3gcuFWy

AetherBorn- The Complete Saga Box Set

https://amzn.to/31tmMYE

ABOUT THE AUTHOR

A.N. Sage has spent most of her life waiting to meet a witch, vampire, or at least get haunted by a ghost. In between failed seances and many questionable outfit choices, she has developed a keen eye for the extra-ordinary.

Since chasing the supernatural does not pay the bills, she dabbled in creative entrepreneurship, marketing and retail management. A.N. spends her free time reading and binge-watching television shows in her pajamas.

Currently, she resides in Toronto, Canada with her husband who is not a creature of the night.

A.N. Sage is a Scorpio and a massive advocate of leggings for pants.

For more books and updates:
www.ansage.ca

Connect on social media:
Facebook Group:

https://www.facebook.com/
groups/945090619339423/

Instagram:
instagram.com/a.n.sage/

Twitter:
twitter.com/ANsageWrites

Facebook:
facebook.com/ansagewrites

Pinterest:
pinterest.ca/ansagewrites

Goodreads:
goodreads.com/author/show/
18901100.Alexis_N_Sage

Amazon:
amazon.com/author/a.n.sage